The Starborn Prince

K. S. Gerlt

Though darkness falls, still the stars find their way.

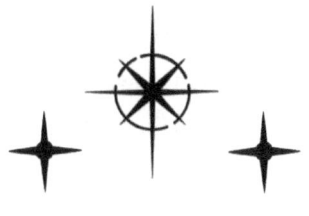

Prologue

"It is a boy, Your Majesty! A beautiful, healthy baby boy." The lady-in-waiting was beaming as she wrapped the wailing newborn in swaddling clothes and gently set him into his mother's arms.

"My little star," she murmured, lovingly running her thin fingers over his mop of dark hair. The queen's own silvery-blonde hair was dampened by perspiration, and despite the dark smudges beneath her light blue eyes, her smile was radiant. "He has his father's hair, already so unruly."

"He has your eyes, my lady."

"He does indeed." The queen's hair glimmered with starlight, which was reflected in the wide eyes of the baby, whose wailing began to ease.

"Have you decided on a name, my lady?" The woman used a dampened cloth to wipe her mistress' brow.

"Sterling. His father and I decided on Sterling."

The queen twirled her fingers in the air, forming the silvery light into miniature stars that danced in the air. The child's crying ceased as he gazed in wonder at the glimmering lights. One of the little stars floated down to rest on the baby's tiny nose, but the moment it touched his skin the light vanished. Immediately, the boy's hair changed from black to a glowing silvery-white before slowly darkening once more.

"My word," the attendant gasped, bringing a hand to her mouth. "It would seem he has inherited far more than just your eyes, Your Majesty."

The queen cradled him close, a look of wonder in her eyes and a soft smile gracing her mouth. She pressed a light kiss to his head, her glow brightening with her joy and turning both of their hair a glowing silvery-white.

"He will be a shining light for all the world to see, my perfect little starborn prince."

Silence reigned for a time, as the newborn's blue eyes fluttered closed, and he fell sound asleep. Only the sound of soft breathing and some faint noises from within the castle disturbed the quiet night air.

"If only Cedric were here to see him," the queen whispered, a touch of sadness in her eyes.

"The King will be so proud of you both when he returns from the desert, Your Majesty," the attendant said comfortingly. "And I have made the arrangements for a starnote to be sent to him immediately with the joyous news."

"Thank you, Esmeray." The queen gave her a tired smile.

"It is my honor and my pleasure, my lady. I shall take my leave so you may rest." The attendant curtsied deeply to her queen, sweeping her skirts to one side. "Please call for me if you have need."

The distant cries grew in volume as they came closer, causing a frown to appear on Esmeray's features. Worry flitted across the queens' drawn face, and her attendant tsked to herself, and mumbled something about incompetent guards.

"Allow me to investigate the commotion, Your Majesty," Esmeray said, and at a nod from her queen, bustled out of the room.

It grew quiet outside, so quiet that the queen's own eyelids began to droop. But a knock at the door startled her awake. Esmeray entered once granted permission, and the troubled expression she wore had the queen sitting up.

"What is the matter, Esmeray?" she asked softly.

"My apologies for disturbing you, Your Majesty. There is a woman here with her daughter, who does not seem long for this world. The woman is refusing to leave until she can plead her case with you, to grant her wish and save her baby girl. I attempted to inform her that you are already exhausted from giving birth and therefore cannot take any visitors, but the woman is in near hysterics."

"How did she encroach so deeply within the castle?" The queen questioned worriedly.

"Though she does not look it, I believe her to be a druid. She must have used her nature magic to enter undetected, until her strength ran out and she was discovered." The attendant paused. "Shall I send her away?"

The queen looked down at the child sleeping in her arms, her eyes softening.

"No. Show her in, but I want guards nearby."

Esmeray curtsied once more before exiting the queen's chambers to speak with the guards outside. Moments later, the attendant led in a bedraggled young woman with dark hair and a sickly complexion, who was clutching a silent bundle to her chest.

"Thank you so much for seeing me, Your Majesty. I am sorry to disturb you, but I am desperate." The woman approached the bed, the flickering candlelight revealing the tear stains on her wind-chapped cheeks, as well as curiously darkened veins. She held out her precious bundle, revealing an infant that was afflicted with the same darkened veins.

The queen's eyes widened when she saw them.

"I have seen this once before. This is no ailment, but the work of a malicious curse, powered by corrupted druid magic. It is a curse of slow decay that feeds upon your own magic. To a newborn, it is a swift death sentence." She cradled the head of her own child, as if to reassure herself he was safe.

"It cannot be...! My father may have been angry, but he would not... he would never..." A choked sob tore from her throat as tears dripped onto her child's pale face, and she fell to her knees as if her strength had wholly abandoned her.

The queen's gaze flickered between the deathly pale baby girl and her own precious newborn, understanding in her pale blue eyes. The queen gestured for her attendant, and handed her the prince after pressing one more kiss to his head. The child stirred, but did not wake.

"Allow me to examine the child," the queen said softly, looking compassionately on the distraught mother.

With trembling hands, the druid woman gave her child to the queen, who held her as gently as she'd held her own. The queen looked closely at the child's face, noting how the girl's breathing grew increasingly labored with each passing moment, and her lips had a bluish tinge.

"She will not last the night without intervention." She met the eyes of the stricken mother. "Though you may last a few years, if you do not use your magic. Spent as I am, I can attempt to seal the girl's magic and stall the curse from progressing, for now. But I am afraid I do not have the strength left in me to completely counter such a powerful curse this night. Once I have recovered, I should be able to do more."

"Thank you! Yes, please, if you can give her just a little more time... It matters not what happens to me! From a mother to a mother, please... Please just save my daughter!" The druid clasped her hands in supplication.

"Then speak your wish, and word it wisely."

"I wish for my daughter's magic to be sealed, so that the curse might be held at bay." Tears of hope and relief flowed freely down her face.

The queen closed her eyes as she began to glow, and silvery starlight poured from the queen and into the child. The little girl cried out and writhed, as if in pain, and the queen's light winked out as the curse drank it in.

The druid's face crumpled.

"Get me starsteel!" The queen ordered as she panted. "I will not give up."

Her attendant quickly snatched one of the queen's own necklaces from her vanity and gave it to her. She placed the star-shaped pendant on the baby's chest, over the center of the darkness, which began to fray apart wherever the starsteel touched. With great effort, the queen's glow returned, and she channeled it into the star pendant and the child before flickering once more.

The queen glanced lovingly and longingly at her little star still sleeping soundly in Esmeray's arms. Then she closed her eyes and pressed her hand into the pendant as her glow intensified into a blinding white, a star descended to earth and given form.

The light filled the room and every being it touched. When it faded, the baby girl was saved, but the queen was gone.

1

Orion

Eyes watched me from the shadows, but I had nothing to fear here. At least, not while I wore the name Orion like protective armor.

The run-down, nondescript home in one neglected corner of the merchant district may not have looked like much, but it served as our main base of operations, and a safe haven for those who were down on their luck. Sometimes, I could count myself among their number.

I quietly rapped my knuckles against the unpainted wooden door, the special pattern of thuds alerting those inside to let me in. Sirius opened the door, but I could tell something was terribly wrong by the look on his face. His warm brown eyes seemed tired, and his sandy-blonde hair stuck out in every direction. His little sister, Estelle, trailed him like a shadow. Her big blue eyes soaked up every detail, despite the late hour.

"What happened?" I asked tersely as I strode inside. Sirius closed and bolted the door behind me.

"One of today's arrivals is stricken with the plague."

"How bad?"

"Bad. She herself did not know, which is why we did not notice the signs immediately. We set her aside, but we have no way of knowing if it spread." Sirous strode purposefully down a dark hall, stopping in front of a door on which hung a sign painted with a black X.

"I will do what I can." He opened the door just long enough for me to slip inside.

"Orion, finally," Astrid said tightly.

Astrid was seated beside the room's sole bed, her long, plaited brown hair hanging over her shoulder as she gently helped her patient to drink. The young girl coughed weakly, but managed to sip the liquid. Dark bruises bloomed on her skin, and the whites of her eyes were tinged with red.

"I came as soon as I could after I saw your starnote." I turned towards the young girl. "How is she?"

"Weakened, but her spirit is strong," Astrid replied for the girl's benefit. She moved over to a table that was pushed against the far wall, where Astrid kept some of her remedies and tools. When I drew close, she whispered, "She is the third case we've seen in the last fortnight. The plague is spreading."

My expression darkened. "Any luck finding an effective remedy?"

"Nothing yet. I can ease her pain, but beyond that..." Astrid trailed off, her hazel eyes shadowed by worry. "At this point, only your miracles can save her."

"Then I will take it from here." I placed a hand on Astrid's shoulder. "Thank you for taking good care of her, Astrid. I know I can always count on you."

A shadow seemed to fall over her face for a moment, but then Astrid gave me a tight smile, and the expression was gone, as if it had never been.

"I do not suppose you will permit me to stay this time?" She narrowed her eyes, but from her stiff posture I could tell she knew what my answer would be.

I winced. Looked away.

"Then I shall take my leave, Guildmaster." Astrid gathered her things, murmured a few words to her patient, and closed the door behind her. I locked it.

I rubbed the back of my neck and heaved a sigh. This had been a recurring argument for almost as long as I had known her, but on this rule I could not budge. The more people who knew my secret, the harder it would be to keep. And I had no doubt that were I discovered, my ability to help these people would be stripped from me immediately.

Besides, trusting others with my secrets had never ended well. Better to keep them close to my chest.

"Hello little lady. My name is Orion. Might I know yours?" I asked as I pulled up a chair beside the bed. Recognition lit in her eyes when she heard my name.

"My name is Mira. Are you really Orion, the Guildmaster of Hyperion?" she whispered in awe, before her thin body was wracked by a coughing fit.

"The one and only," I replied with an easy smile.

"They say that if the Guildmaster sees to you personally, you're guaranteed to be delivered from any peril." Mira's eyes turned glassy. "Can you really save me?"

"I will certainly try my best, but it all depends on you, Mira. Can you keep a very important secret?" I leaned forward, wearing a serious but not unkind expression.

"Yes, of course!" Mira nodded eagerly. Her blonde bangs flopped with the motion.

"Very good. In order for me to help you, I need you to say out loud that you wish to be healthy and whole, now and for the rest of your days. The wording is very important." I saw uncertainty in her eyes at my words, and expected her next question.

"I...are you asking me to give up my wish as payment?" Mira frowned, and lifted her starsteel wish pendant from where it rested on her chest.

"Not at all. Your wish is yours to use at one of the festivals," I reassured her. "I am asking you to make a wish, so that I may grant it now to save you. It will not be officially recognized as your one wish."

"But I thought only the king could grant wishes, during the quarterly Wish Festival."

"That is why I need you to keep this a secret, Mira. Can you do that for me?" I placed my hand over her smaller one, letting a glimmer of starlight dance through the air between us.

Her eyes widened, and she nodded again.

"Thank you, Mira. Now, remember what I said earlier? Repeat it back to me, word for word." I hated that it had come to this, that I was forced to use my last resort. I braced myself for the pain I knew was coming.

"I wish to be healthy and whole for the rest of my days," she recited, her trusting eyes never once leaving mine.

A strained smile hovered on my lips as I closed my eyes and guided the pure power of starlight from the star sapphire amulet that was concealed beneath my tunic, down my arm, through my fingers, and into Mira. She and I both began to glow with a bright silvery light, miniature stars whirling around us, but I continued drawing power from the amulet until the starlight had completely healed her, and burned away any lingering traces of infection. Blinding light filled the room, bright even through my closed eyelids. I made sure that a small kernel of starlight would stay with her always, to protect her just as she had wished.

I felt the burning in my back that signified the wish had been fully granted, but I kept my expression smooth. I finally allowed the starlight to fade away, and withdrew my hand.

I had been granting far too many wishes as of late.

Mira lifted her hands and arms before her, examining them closely for the dark bruises that had marred her skin mere moments before, but her skin was now clear. Tears welled in her clear green eyes and spilled down her cheeks, and before I could say anything, she leaped into my arms.

"Thank you. Thank you, Orion! Your secret is safe with me, always."

I stroked her back comfortingly, even as her fingers caused the pain in my back to flare stronger. I grit my teeth. A little pain was a small price to pay for her life.

When I was little, I learned the terrible truth that wishes are never free to those who grant them. And sometimes, the price was more than we could pay. Because the king kept this truth a secret, the line of wish-seekers was never-ending. That was why I had formed this guild in secret, to try to wean the people of Astoria off of their reliance on the magic of the stars.

But every now and then, like tonight, that beautiful and deadly power was the only thing standing between life and death.

After a few murmured words of comfort, I was able to extricate myself from Mira's tight grip. "Get some rest, little star. You are safe here." I tucked her in and blew out the candle before I left the room, closing the door softly behind me.

I paused as I passed the next room down, where Astrid was busily splinting a careless child's sprained ankle. What must have been the boy's mother hovered anxiously, fidgeting like a frantic comet. I leaned against the doorframe, folding my arms over my chest. Fatigue pulled at me as a sweets-maker pulled taffy, just as surely as it must be pulling at Astrid. Yet here she was, a seemingly bottomless well of energy.

Her devotion to the guild never failed to inspire me. Hyperion had been able to help many more people than I would have ever imagined thanks to her. It was my hope that her ingenious remedies and treatments could someday replace wish-granting entirely.

As if she sensed my gaze, Astrid half-turned to glance at me. She quirked an eyebrow, as if to ask why my hands were idle. I grinned. Astrid rolled her eyes and finished attending to her young patient, and gave the anxious mother an ointment and some instructions before she came over to me.

"Is there anyone else in dire need tonight?" I asked, suppressing a yawn. I sincerely hoped not.

Astrid must have seen the fatigue in my face, however, because her eyes softened. "No, not tonight. The rest can be treated through ordinary remedies and plenty of rest."

I sagged in relief.

"There is nothing ordinary about your methods." Astrid smiled at the compliment. "If that is the case, I think I will retire for the night."

Astrid's smile fell. "So soon? You only just arrived."

"I know." I sighed, pinching the bridge of my nose. "But if I am going to get everything done tomorrow and still stop by the guild, I cannot pull another all-nighter."

"Can I help lighten the load of your...what is your day trade, again?" Astrid asked in a suspiciously nonchalant tone.

"Nice try. You know I cannot say." I smiled sadly, my heart heavy with the weighted boulder of my secret. Astrid was surely used to my secrecy by now, but that did not stop her from occasionally trying to catch me off-guard. "But...please send me a starnote if you encounter any more plague victims."

"I will." Her eyes shuttered at my soft rejection. I hated when she looked at me like that. But it was for her sake, and for everyone elses' that I had to keep my lips sealed. "I had hoped that if we caught it early, we could prevent it from spreading, but..." She bit her lip. "Orion, this sickness...it is like nothing I have ever seen before. None of my typical remedies are effective against it."

I scowled, tapping a finger against my forearm. A sickness even Astrid could not treat...that posed a huge problem. If the only surefire cure was the power of the amulet I wore...my plans would be ruined. "Ask Noctus to search for any who show symptoms, and have him bring them to the black X room. I will see to as many as I can."

It would be a problem if this thing spread—after all, there were limits to how many wishes I could grant in a single night. At least, without severe, if not deadly, consequences. Better to nip it in the bud.

"Understood." Astrid looked back towards the mother and son for a moment, a wistful look glazing her eyes. "There are more and more every day, and with this plague... The king simply is not granting wishes fast enough."

"The next Wish Festival is just weeks away," I offered. Even though the celebration lasted a full week, the king was only ever able to grant a handful of wishes each night. Even granting those few always carried the possibility that I would lose him, too. But if this new sickness spread...

"From what I have seen, this plague kills quickly. Those struck by it now will not live to see the festival." Astrid turned her gaze to mine, and I could not help but wonder if her gaze would be filled with accusation if she knew who I was during the day.

"The king may have to expand the capacity of the emergency wish ministry. Either way, Hyperion will have to fill in the gaps." After all, if we could split this burden, it reduced the risk of either of us burning out. I gave her a lop-sided grin. "Which means you will be seeing much more of me."

"No one in the guild would complain about that," Astrid said warmly. Then she paused, concern filling her eyes. "I know you never get sick, but...please be careful."

I smiled, and put a hand on her shoulder. "I will. You be careful as well. If any guild member so much as sneezes, I want to know about it. Though darkness falls..."

Astrid nodded. "Still the stars find their way." Some emotion I could not name flickered in the depths of her molten hazel eyes, and for a moment I thought she had something more to say. Instead, she briefly placed her hand over mine, like a butterfly alighting on a flower, before she turned and went to attend to her next patient.

The cobblestone streets were dark and silent as I made my way back through the heart of Astoria. Only the cold and distant stars kept me company as I made the long walk back home.

I nodded my head at the maid who curtsied to me as I made my way through the carpeted halls and back to my rooms. She greeted me politely as I passed.

"Good evening, Prince Sterling."

2

Astrid

"**N**ext, use your mortar and pestle to crush the elderberry to extract the juice," I instructed my class of eager students.

I demonstrated the motion for them, and the crisp morning air was soon filled with the sound of stone grinding against stone. I kept an eye on my motley group of pupils as they worked, happy to see both new and returning faces. People from all walks of life came to attend my classes. Wealthy merchants sat beside orphans, and busy housewives worked next to elderly grandfathers.

One of the apothecaries with whom Hyperion maintained close relations lent us their back room once a week. Of course, they were also happy to sell me the materials for each class, and I sweetened the deal by handing over a case of my own bottled remedies at no additional charge. The location for the class changed every month, to ensure that those from all corners of the city had the chance to attend.

The small fee each attendee paid was not enough to cover even the cost of the materials, but profit was not the point of these little sessions. They were a part of Orion's grand plan, his vision of an Astoria filled with people who relied on themselves, instead of the king and his wishes, to solve their problems.

Through some trial and error in the beginning, we had learned that offering free classes was not the best way to go about it. If the classes were free, then materials would mysteriously disappear, students would show up late or not at all, and they often had a less-than-eager attitude towards learning. It was unfortunate, but most people only valued what they had to pay for—even if it was only a nominal fee.

"Do we add in the ginger next?" asked Nova, one of my favorite students. She was an orphan from the same charitable home as me, but her boundless optimism reassured me that her future would be bright. She would make it so.

She reminded me of myself in that regard.

"No, next is the mint," corrected Castor, Nova's closest friend. The pair were inseparable. Wherever Nova went, he was sure to follow.

"You are both correct," I said with a warm smile. "Scrape the paste into your mixing bowl, and then we will be working both ginger root and mint leaves into a paste."

Nova stuck her tongue out at Castor, who flicked the tip of her nose in response. I chuckled quietly to myself at the teenagers' antics. The other students seemed just as entertained by the pair as I. They attended almost every one of my classes, and their bright spirits always livened up the atmosphere.

"After you have added the paste to your bowl, it is time to add some honey." I eyed Nova. "And no eating the honey, or there will not be enough for the remedy!"

Nova pouted, her mischievous freckles pulled down in a scowl. Castor pulled her fiery red hair back from her face as it fell dangerously close to her remedy as she poured it into the jar, and she smiled gratefully at him.

My thoughts briefly strayed to Orion, and I wondered what he was up to this morning. Perhaps he was the son of a wealthy merchant, and he was busy minding the store, or even keeping his father's books. Or perhaps he was patrolling Astor Castle as one its guards, or even as one of its elite Knights of the Evening Star, which were formerly the late queen's guards.

A sudden clatter startled me from my daydreaming. Terry, a kind older man, was staring forlornly at his overturned mixture, which was now dripping onto the floor. He clenched his unsteady hands in frustration, and the housewife next to him jumped into action to mop up the spill.

"How foolish of me. Thank you, Sally, for your help," he told the housewife.

"Think nothing of it, dear." She had the mess cleaned up in a flash. While she worked, I added honey to my own mixture and then poured it into a glass jar that I stopped with a cork.

"I want you to have mine, Terry," I said as I stood and walked over to him. I set the jar in front of him.

"I—I thank you, Astrid, but I cannot possibly accept," he said sadly.

"I know you came to make a remedy for your granddaughter," I replied softly. "Please, take it for her."

He closed a trembling hand around the glass, as if it were the most precious thing in the world. "Thank you."

"Anytime." I returned to my seat at the head of the table to address the rest of the class. "Thank you all for coming today. I will be hosting one more class in this location before moving to another apothecary a short walk from here. I sincerely hope that this common cold remedy you have learned today will bless you and your families."

The students thanked me before leaving, but I caught Nova and Castor before they headed back to the orphanage. Keeping my eyes on Terry as he shuffled out the door, I whispered, "If you go with Terry and help him administer that to his granddaughter, I will waive both of your fees for the next class."

Nova's eyes lit up. "Consider it done!"

Castor nodded solemnly, and the pair soon caught up with Terry. A smile curved my lips as I watched Nova offer to carry the precious jar for him, and Castor loop his arm through the older gentleman's, to help him walk. The boy's hair shone like a freshly polished gold coin as he stepped into the sun. Nova could be a little too energetic at times, but with Castor by her side, I had no doubt they would see their mission through.

"All done for the day?" breathed a quiet voice in my ear.

I jumped in surprise, my hand automatically reaching for an arrow from a quiver that was not on my back. My bow and quiver lay on a table across the room. But before panic set in, I recognized the man standing beside me.

"Noctus! Quit doing that!" I whisper-shouted at him, pressing a hand to my frantic heart.

"Your reactions are far too entertaining for me to quit." An amused smile hovered on his lips. His dark eyes, hair, and clothes blended perfectly into the shadows he so enjoyed hiding in. It would not surprise me in the least if he had the ability to dive into his own shadow, as well.

"Hmph. No dinner for you, then." I crossed my arms over my chest, pretending to pout.

"Fine, fine, I apologize. You know I cannot resist your cooking," he relented sheepishly. "How about I help you clean up to make up for it?"

"Deal." I smirked when he realized I had only been pretending, but he still cleaned off the work table in record time. "Has Sirius finished with his swordsmanship class?"

"Yes and no." Noctus rolled his eyes. "The class is over, but he insisted on staying late to spar with two of his students."

"How like him." He would be getting an earful from his little sister for being late, though.

"Since I was already in the area investigating an unfaithful husband for a client, I thought I might walk you home," Noctus said as he put the last jar away.

But I narrowed my eyes. "What brought this on? I know you usually prefer to avoid the crowded streets at this time of day."

"Well…" Noctus looked away, and I knew I had hit the bullseye. At my raised eyebrow, he finally relented. "Lately, I have been hearing of some…unsavory characters in the area."

I slowly slung my bow and quiver over my back. If Noctus was worried enough that he had come to escort me himself, the situation was worse than he was letting on. Especially considering his fear of crowded places.

"Thank you." I smiled up at him and looped my arm through his proffered one. I had no siblings of my own, but I imagined this was what it would feel like to have a protective older brother. My heart warmed at the thought.

As we made our way through the packed cobblestone streets, I kept my eyes and ears open. And whenever someone caught Noctus' attention, I would follow his gaze. That was when it truly hit me how many more desert tribesmen and women I saw.

It was not uncommon to occasionally see one of the brightly-dressed and veiled women going about her daily errands, but now that I was looking, I noticed scores of them. Some were interacting with the Astorians, bartering for bread and vegetables, but most congregated on street corners, their hands upraised in supplication.

Since when had there been so many tribeswomen in Astoria?

And despite their prostrate posture while begging for coin, why did their dark-eyed gazes feel so unsettling?

3

Orion

"What were you up to last night, Your Highness?" grunted Sir Rigel, the knight with whom I was sparring. He had taken over training me from his father for the past few years, ever since his father had become the king's personal knight and Rigel had officially joined the Order of the Evening Star. He was a handful of years older than me, and he was the closest thing I had to a brother.

"What do you mean?" My pulse spiked, but I kept my features blank as I blocked his strike.

"I spotted you wandering around the halls, long after I would have expected you to retire for the evening. Since you were swathed in a cloak, I nearly mistook you for an intruder until

I spotted your sword." He kept his tone light, but I could sense the unspoken question there.

"I had difficulty sleeping, so I decided to get some fresh air." I went on the attack, hoping both my words and my practice sword would distract him.

"And the disguise?" he huffed, his blade cracking against mine.

He parried my blows, and I used the recoil to bring my wooden sword around in a precise arc, whacking the knight's sword arm with the flat of the blade. Before he could recover, I snaked my sword around his and flung it from his grasp, and brought the tip of my wooden weapon to rest an inch away from his throat.

"I simply did not wish to be disturbed while doing so," I replied as I lowered the point of my sword.

"Is that so? In that case, I might recommend disguising yourself as a servant, instead. Far less noticeable that way. But if we continue sparring every morning, I would be surprised if you still have trouble sleeping." He lowered the point of my sword with a finger. "You have improved greatly, Your Highness." Rigel retrieved his wooden practice sword and offered me a slight bow.

"Thank you, Sir Rigel. Though I will have to train diligently if I want to prevail against you with any consistency." I smiled warmly.

"Care for another round?" The knight flourished his sword with an ease I strove to emulate.

"Another time, perhaps," I said as I handed him my sword, so he could return it to its place. "My father is expecting me."

"Very well, Prince Sterling. Until next time." Rigel bowed as I gave him a wave and exited the training hall to head deeper into the castle.

I wiped the sweat from my brow with the hem of my tunic. I laughed at myself when I realized I was attempting to do so without uncovering the skin of my back as a force of habit. So long as the sun was above the horizon, I did not have to fear another spying the constellations inked in starlight on my skin.

After nightfall, however, it was a different story. But by then, I was usually away from castle grounds or holed up in my room. I chuckled. That also seemed to be the source of a rumor I had heard, that the prince was too sickly or inept to set foot outside. Far better to be taken for an incompetent fool than suffer my father's wrath if he learned what I truly did at night.

Would I ever have the courage to tell him? It seemed the longer I put it off, the more I had to lose if he found out.

I squared my shoulders and stopped by my rooms to splash some water on my face and change my attire to something a tad more presentable. I double-checked in the mirror that the star sapphire amulet was not visible beneath my clothes before I left my rooms. Then I made my way through the castle and to the innermost keep, where the king's study and personal library were located.

I grinned when I spotted Sir Magnus Gallahad, Rigel's father and the king's personal knight, standing guard at the door.

According to my father, he had been serving our family ever since my mother saved his life, when they were all young and seeking a place better than Harland to settle. He had been a faithful knight ever since, and I could always tell if my father was in a room by his presence.

"How long has he been holed up in there this time?" I asked as I approached.

"Long enough for my legs to fall asleep," he groused, though his twitching mustache gave away his slight smile. "I would be much obliged if you could convince him to see the sun every now and again."

"I make no promises," I chuckled as he announced my arrival. It still felt strange to banter with the knight so freely—the man's sense of humor evaporated on the training field. But it was thanks to him I had learned how to properly wield a sword.

"Enter," came a muffled voice from within. Sir Magnus opened the door for me, and I nodded my thanks as I stepped inside.

I took a moment to breathe in the familiar scent of musty parchment and leather that filled the space, which was warmed by the crackling fire. My father's desk was situated directly across from the fire, above which hung a portrait of my mother. She smiled down at us softly, her silvery hair and eyes almost seeming to glow in the darkness. Instead of expensive fabrics being arrayed behind her in the background, the artist had painted a night sky filled with stars.

Bookcases stuffed to the brim lined the rest of the walls, though not a speck of dust marred them. When I was little, I wondered why my father was so keen on a room without any windows, since it always seemed so dark and dreary to me. But now, I understood how this place had become his sanctuary.

Just as Hyperion had become mine.

The king was seated at his desk, and despite my entrance, his eyes remained fixated on the portrait of the late queen. Although he generally accomplished his work in a timely manner, I always wondered exactly how much time he spent gazing upon her portrait. If it were not for his many duties as king, he might have never left this room.

"You called for me, Sovereign Father?" I cleared my throat, and my father finally tore his amber eyes away from the painting.

"Dispense with the formalities, you rascal," he growled at me, but the effect was dampened by his broad smile. "Sterling, come and sit with me."

"But you are far too fun to tease." I obliged, and sat in one of the comfortable leather chairs that faced the fire.

My father got up from his desk and sat across from me. As much as I loved the comforting smokey scent of the fire, I detested how the flickering light made the deep lines in my father's face so much more pronounced. The silver at his temples certainly did not help, either.

"Tell me, son, how fares the kingdom? I do wish I had the leisure time to leave the castle more often." The king leaned forward slightly in his chair.

"It has been better, I am afraid," I replied evenly. As far as he knew, my weekly patrols with the guards in town were my only visits there—and I needed to keep it that way.

I kept my face impassive, despite the way my heart had jumped at the question. If my father knew exactly how frequently I left the castle without guards, my reception would have been far different.

"How so?" He frowned.

"Well, I am sure you have received reports of the spread of a new plague recently," I began slowly, but was interrupted.

"Plague?! Was it not the usual few cases of springtime illness that we get every year?" he questioned with a frown.

I blinked. Had the severity of this threat not been understood by the council? Or had it been glossed over purposefully?

"It is a sickness unlike any we have ever seen before. None of the apothecaries' usual remedies have any effect, and so far, most cases have been fatal," I answered grimly. "And it is spreading."

"Perhaps we should postpone the upcoming Wish Festival to prevent it from spreading," he murmured, stroking his beard as if deep in thought.

"No!" He looked at me in surprise. "No, canceling or postponing the festival would only make things worse. I suspect most of the upcoming wishes will be to save loved ones from this plague, and so postponing it would cause great unrest in Astoria."

"You do have a point." He narrowed his eyes on me. "What would you suggest, prince?" I stiffened at his use of my title.

"It would be wise to fund research for a cure, and to consider delegating some of the emergency wish granting..." I trailed off, choosing my words carefully. He was testing me, and I knew what answer he was looking for, but it was an answer I could not give. "To me."

"Absolutely not!" he roared, half-rising from his seat. "That is the one burden I refuse to relinquish!"

"Some of our people are starting to think that I am incapable of it—that Astoria will be doomed by a magicless prince," I said, feeling resentful but resigned to my fate, to the very magic that stole my mother from me. "Some even question whether I am truly the son of a fallen star."

"What nonsense! Surely you take after me most strongly, but...you have your mother's eyes, if not her innate powers." He scowled, clearly agitated.

"The people will only grow more worried about Astoria's future the longer you insist on bearing this responsibility alone," I argued. As much as I appreciated how he had tried to shield me from this risk, I also worried that the day would come when it claimed him, too. But if we shared that risk...perhaps it would lessen for the both of us.

"Eventually, I will teach you to use the amulet." He sighed heavily.

"When, exactly, will that be? Let me help you! Let me use the amulet Mother made for us, to help—" I pleaded, but my father cut me off.

"No!" he shouted, the sudden outburst echoing against the walls. "No. You know why... You know exactly why I cannot let you do that. It is far too risky, and I refuse to lose you, too. Not the same way we lost your mother. I, at least, know how much magic I can draw from the amulet before it will start consuming my lifeforce instead of starlight."

I gritted my teeth, just barely stopping myself from blurting out that I was well aware of where that line was. "How am I meant to lessen your burden, to learn how to use it if you only ever permit me to recharge the amulet with liquid starlight?"

My father went quiet, his expression softening. "We have been over this a thousand times, Sterling," he finally said. "Why are you so adamant about this?"

"Because...I am afraid of losing you, too. Because someday, I want to be as great a king as you are! Because I want our people to be able to have faith in me, to rely on me!" I wanted to put their minds at ease with a public display of competence, and I wanted to quit lying to my own father about the half of my life I had kept from him all these years. It had been fun and exciting at first, leading this double life. But lately...it felt like my secrets were starting to cause more harm than good. They were like a weight tied to my ankles, hobbling me like a horse tied to a stake.

"The people had faith in your mother, and look what happened to her," he said bitterly. "Hesperia gave everything she had, and it was still not enough."

"I have no intention of leaving you alone, Father. Or allowing you to leave me and join her," I said softly. "I just...want to make you both proud." And eventually, to do away with wish-granting entirely.

At the look on my face, he sank back into his leather chair, rubbing his temples. "And I respect that. But can you understand my reasoning?"

"I understand, even if I disagree," I said with a dejected sigh. My eyes strayed to her portrait. How different things would be if she were still here.

The king sighed wearily.

"Your first proposal, however, does have merit," he admitted slowly, his eyes softening when he saw where I was looking. "I did not want to burden you, but since you keep asking for more responsibility... I will put you in charge of managing the development of a cure. In addition, I would like you to oversee the upcoming Wish Festival. I realize I have put this off for far too long. But you are right—it is far past time for me to pass on my knowledge to you. And there is no better teacher than experience." He patted my hand.

"I—thank you, father. I promise I will not disappoint you." It sounded as if Father still intended to bear the burden of granting the wishes himself, but this was certainly a good start.

"You never could, my boy." A lump rose in my throat. I hated the way I doubted his words. If he knew what I had been up to in secret for so long, could he still say the same?

"I..." I trailed off, my secrets hovering on the tip of my tongue. But instead, I simply said, "Thank you, Father."

"You have grown into such a fine young man, Sterling." His gaze drifted back to the portrait, as if drawn by a magnet. "I am certain she must be smiling down on you."

"On *us*, Father," I said around the sudden lump in my throat. "You have been a wonderful king."

"I try my best," he said with a sigh. "You know, never in my wildest dreams did I imagine that one day I would be a king. I was actually quite hesitant at first."

I blinked.

"You were?" This was news to me.

"Your mother was the one that people truly adored. She just had this way with others, a charm not even the surliest hermit could resist." The king chuckled, a wistful look entering his amber eyes.

"And...were you that hermit?" I asked with a slight smile.

"Guilty as charged." His smile widened. "When the people who had flocked to her began to worship her as a deity, it made her incredibly uncomfortable. But they insisted on showing her their respect and gratitude for all she had done for them, and so she became their queen, instead."

"And that made you their king," I murmured.

He nodded.

"That made me their king. I objected at first, but...it brought my dear Hesperia so much joy to grant other's wishes, and I came to see that having more people around to help me protect her was not such a terrible thing. We never expected our northern sanctuary to become such a large kingdom so quickly."

"You never wanted to be a king?" I asked, surprised.

"No. But I did want to honor my wife's wishes, and help and protect the people who came to Astoria. Many of them became like family to us. And though more people arrived than we could possibly help in a lifetime of trying, we did our best." His eyes turned glassy. "And I have done my utmost to continue my love's legacy ever since."

I stood up and walked over to my father, and placed a hand on his shoulder. He had rarely been so open with me like this before, and I could not help but feel my own eyes begin to mist. It made my heart ache, and I wished more than anything that I could have had the chance to know my mother, beyond the stories I had been told.

But even the strongest wish could not return those who were already lost to us.

"I think she would be proud of everything you have accomplished in her name," I said around the lump in my throat. He put his hand over mine, and both of our gazes returned to the portrait.

Eventually, my father cleared his throat, gave my hand a pat, and stood to return to his desk. I walked with him, but all thoughts of my mother fled when I spied the reports that were waiting for him. I skimmed them quickly, trying not to be too obvious as the king took a seat.

"I will have the documents pertaining to researching a cure drawn up and on your desk for your approval in the next few days. I will begin consulting with the festival committees as well. And please, Father..." I looked him in the eye. "Let me know if there is anything more I can do to ease your burden."

"I appreciate the offer, Sterling. I will give it some thought," he replied, his eyes softening.

I bowed my head respectfully and left his study, my thoughts already racing ahead of me. I mindlessly made my way back to my own study, which was in a little-used tower that had the most stunning view of the night sky, thanks to the windows that made up one entire wall.

I closed the door behind me and sank into my favorite chair, which faced the bank of windows, so I could look out across Astoria. My lips thinned. The reports on my father's desk had been mostly from the borders. The soldiers stationed there all gave their accounts of increasingly frequent skirmishes with druids, witches, and desert tribesmen. There had been few casualties, but they were requesting both reinforcements and a fresh supply of starsteel weapons, since the special metal was their only true defense against the various magics employed by those who sought to either harass or enter the kingdom.

The druids were particularly tricky, as they could command both plants and animals to attack on their behalf. How did one fight a tree, or a swarm of bees? At least most of the witches' hexes wore off within a few hours, but the only way to stop rampaging trees and vines was to eliminate the druid controlling them with a starsteel blade.

It seemed we would soon be fighting on two fronts, with these frequent skirmishes at the border and an emerging plague within. Finding that cure now held even more importance than ever before.

I pulled out my starsteel watch and a small bottle of liquid starlight. I uncorked the stopper and allowed a few drops of the precious substance to fall onto the inner mirror of the watch's lid. The starsteel absorbed the silvery drops and began to hum and glow. Quickly, I wrote out a few lines and sent the starnote to Astrid's watch.

If anyone could come up with a cure, it was her.

I snapped the watch closed and returned it to my pocket before I summoned my attendant, Zale.

"Prince Sterling, I see you have returned from your morning practice with the knights. Should I send for some ice?" Zale asked once he arrived.

"I will have you know I won three out of five rounds today," I said with mock outrage. "But if you require ice after another rejection from Sienna, please feel free to send for some."

"Touché, Highness, touché," Zale sighed dramatically. "I will win her affections yet, just you wait and see."

"Whatever you say, Zale," I said with a laugh, and Zale joined in good-naturedly. "In all seriousness, though, I need you to pull some records for me while I draft a new proposal."

"Understood, Highness." He took the list I held out, nodded, and left with a bow.

I turned my gaze back to the cloudless blue sky. If I were being honest with myself, the idea of overseeing the Wish Festival while also searching for a cure terrified me. I had never been responsible for something so important before—at least, not in an official capacity as the prince.

If things went well, if I proved myself to my father... Perhaps then I might work up the courage to tell him about the guild I had created, and how I had been trying to continue my mother's legacy in my own way. Even if it meant going against his wishes.

4

Orion

The sun was setting as I slipped into town, the golden rays painting the sky with ruby tones. I took my time as I strolled through the bustling streets on my way to my favorite tavern. I enjoyed the savory aroma of grilling meat and cooking vegetables that floated in the air, and the sound of laughing children who were playing one last game before being called in to dinner.

Turning a corner, my steps slowed. A young and striking tribeswoman knelt in front of a small child, whose hair was matted and whose clothes were tattered and patched. The young girl hesitantly accepted a loaf of bread from the foreigner, whose long, dark hair contrasted starkly against her bright red and orange garments. It fell in loose waves down her back, and I wondered if her lack of a veil meant she had begun to adopt the culture of my people.

The rapid clatter of horseshoes on stone caught my attention, and I looked up to see a carriage careening out of control down the street. The bay horse's eyes were rolling in its head, and foam bubbled at its mouth. The carriage it pulled veered erratically to either side of the street, forcing people to leap out of its path. The coachman was nowhere to be seen, and the horse was barreling straight towards the tribeswoman and child, who had yet to notice the approaching danger.

"Look out!" I cried as I leaped into motion. The young woman looked up in surprise, and pulled the child into her arms as she tried to move out of the way.

But she was not going to make it in time.

I put on a burst of speed, pushing my legs to work faster, despite their stiffness from a morning spent sparring. Just before the horse reached the pair, I lunged for the reins. I thanked the stars when my hand closed around the leather strip, and I used all the strength I could muster to haul the horse's head around, so that its nose was nearly touching its shoulder. The woman ducked into a side alley as the carriage swung around in an arc, and I brought the horse to an abrupt halt.

The poor animal's chest heaved, and sweat streaked its sides. It pranced in place, but so long as I kept its head pointed backwards, it would not be able to run forward. It flinched and shuddered as I ran a hand along its neck comfortingly, my own chest heaving from exertion. It tried to shy away from me, so I ran a critical eye over the animal and its harness.

In no time, I spotted the problem: a metal buckle had been bent out of shape, and a sharp point had dug into the poor animal's side, thanks to the heavy weight of the improperly attached harness.

Keeping one hand on the reins, I carefully moved to the horse's side and pulled out the offending metal in one swift motion. The prancing immediately ceased, and when I loosened my hold, the poor animal's head drooped down nearly to the cobblestones as it panted, its legs trembling.

Those who had darted into hiding slowly emerged, and many began to applaud when they saw the horse was now under control. What must have been the coachman came jogging towards me, his slovenly appearance a reflection of his slovenly work.

"Thank you, good sir," the pot-bellied man gasped as he came up to me. I wrinkled my nose at the foul stink of alcohol that wafted from him. "I am most grateful for your timely assistance." When he went to take the reins from me, I jerked them just out of reach.

"Your carelessness could have cost someone their life," I bit out.

"I beg your pardon?!" He drew up short, looking indignant. "The nag spooked out of nowhere, and just took off—"

I shoved the broken bit of metal, still coated with crimson, in the man's face. "I would like to see *you* maintain *your* composure with a nail driving into your ribs."

The man paled as the people around us began to murmur angrily.

"Animal abuse is not tolerated in Astoria," I announced loudly for those around us to hear. "Nor is drinking while driving a carriage."

The man sputtered, his face turning scarlet.

I pulled the man's hand forward, depositing both the metal and the reins into it. I leaned closer, so only he could hear, and whispered, "This is your one and only warning. Should I hear that anything like this ever happens again, the royal guards will be the least of your worries."

His sputtering ceased when I rested my hand on my sword. He swallowed, nodded mutely, and went about his business with his head hung low.

Now that that was taken care of, I nodded to those who called out their thanks and approached the tribeswoman, who was just setting the child back on her feet. As she stood and turned towards me, the setting sun caught her dark eyes just right, turning them to pools of amber-gold. Those mesmerizing eyes held mine as her deep red lips curved in a smile. Her sun-kissed face was perfectly framed by her sun-gilded locks, and I found myself staring, transfixed by her beauty.

"Thank you for your help." Her voice was rich like honey, and the intoxicating perfume she wore smelled just as sweet.

"Thank you, mister," added the young girl, who still clutched her bread to her chest.

"Are you both unhurt?" I asked, coming back to my senses.

"Yes, fortunately. Your warning came just in time." The tribeswoman glanced down at the child, as if checking once more for injuries.

"Mister, you must be really strong." The girl's eyes were wide with curiosity.

I chuckled. "I simply know my way around a horse. That one did not mean to hurt anybody—it just had a nasty thorn in its side, and needed someone to take it out."

The girl nodded sagely, gave me a cheeky smile, and then scampered off without so much as a goodbye.

"Thank you for helping that child." I ran a hand through my hair, suddenly feeling self-conscious. "May I ask for your name?'

"My name is Nyra. And if I might be so bold, would you allow me to treat my savior to a meal, Mr...?" she trailed off expectantly.

"Orion. And I would be delighted—I know just the place." I held out my arm, and after just a moment of hesitation, she took it.

I was so distracted on the way that I nearly walked right past the tavern, The Wandering Comet. But I held the door open for her, and returned the greetings that were thrown my way by a few familiar patrons. I showed Nyra to a quieter table towards the back of the small but clean tavern before I sidled up to the bar.

One of the reasons I frequented this particular tavern was to listen to the concerns and triumphs of the locals. As Orion, I could discover exactly what was troubling them, without either the sugar-coating or anger that

Prince Sterling would receive. The other reason was that I had become quite close with the tavern's owner and barkeep, Ace.

"Good to see you, Orion," Ace greeted me warmly.

He leaned against the bar as he idly polished a glass, his brawny arms flexing with each motion. His muscular physique, combined with his bald head and magnificent mustache, were intimidating enough to discourage any brawls before they began. The man had no qualms about giving overly-rowdy patrons the boot.

"Good to be here," I replied easily. "How about two tankards of mead and two bowls of stew for me and...my acquaintance over there?"

Ace's bushy eyebrows shot towards his shining crown. "Acquaintance, eh? Astrid will be thrilled," he muttered so quietly I nearly missed it. Louder, he said, "Coming right up." He filled two tankards and slid them over to me, palming the gold coin I slipped him.

"Anything noteworthy to report?" I murmured quietly, choosing to ignore his commentary on my company.

"The usual mutterings. Although...there have been rumblings about a deadly sickness cropping up here and there, as well as some...dissatisfaction, shall we say."

I frowned. "Dissatisfaction?"

Ace leaned closer. "I have heard tell of some of those foreigners riling up the locals, with talk of how the king should be granting more wishes."

"Let me guess—the foreigners want their own wishes to be granted?" I raised an eyebrow.

"Most likely," Ace grunted. "Of course, that is not how they phrase it. But I doubt they would be raising such a fuss for any other reason."

I scowled. These foreigners were threatening my entire plan with their vocal dissent and their ignorance. If such vitriol spread, it would become harder than ever to encourage people to rely on themselves instead of on wishes. After all, it was a far more risky undertaking to think for yourself, as opposed to waiting to be told what to do, or for your dream to be handed to you on a silver platter.

But Astoria and her people would never become all that they could be, so long as this debilitating reliance remained. And I would forever be haunted by the possibility of losing my father as well, so long as it did.

"Keep up the good work." I nodded to Ace as I grabbed the tankards and joined Nyra at the table.

The smell of her sweet perfume cut through even the sharp scent of alcohol that permeated the room. My worries from just moments before began to melt away, dripping from my mind like water through a loosely-woven basket.

"This was meant to be my treat," Nyra purred as she took a sip of her drink, her dark eyes glued to mine over the rim.

"I never make a woman pay." Her expression froze, and I hurried to add, "At least, not one who took such good care of a child you had only just met. Especially when you were both in grave danger. Most would have saved themselves, but you protected the girl."Nyra's expression thawed, and I breathed a silent sigh of relief. I had nearly forgotten how possessive and controlling tribesmen were of their women, and I certainly did not want to come across as such.

"I know what it is to lose someone you hold dear," she said sadly, her eyes downcast. "If I could easily save the girl but chose not to, I could not bear the shame."

"That is an admirable sentiment." I took a sip of my own drink, and feeling emboldened, added, "I am sorry for your loss. Losing someone you love is...far more painful than any physical wound."

Her dark, mesmerizing eyes lifted to mine, her lips parting in surprise. "At least physical wounds heal with time. But forgetting that pain, allowing it to fade...that would dishonor her memory."

"Does your loss have to do with why you have come to Astoria?" The raw pain in her voice, in her depthless eyes, made me think that her loss was far more recent than mine. I knew we had only just met, but there was just something about this woman that pulled on my heartstrings. It may have been presumptuous of me, but I hoped that airing her story would help bring her some measure of solace.

"In a way, yes." She bit her lip, hesitating, before rushing on, "My older sister, Farah, was so full of joy and kindness. I was happy for her when she became the third wife of the Gorata Chieftain. But theirs was the first oasis to dry up. By the time I heard the news and traveled there from the Akangli tribelands with what little water we could spare..."

Nyra trailed off, tears forming at the corners of her eyes. She looked up, as if to keep them from falling. I placed my hand over hers comfortingly, and she gave me a weak smile.

She took a shuddering breath, and continued, "The Chief had hoarded the remaining water, giving it only to his first two wives and their male children. His little girls were cast aside, and my sister, who had been with child...she died in my arms, a dried-up husk of her former self."

I squeezed her hand. "How terrible." Farah's tragic tale gave me a newfound appreciation that my father had banned such polygamous customs in Astoria.

"My tribe's oasis began to dry up soon after." She wiped discreetly at the corners of her eyes, and I rubbed soothing circles on her soft skin. "And so I journeyed here, to the land where wishes can be made real, in the hope that I might save my people."

I stilled, resisting the urge to recoil from another supplicant who came seeking an easy solution to her problem. An easy solution that could cost me my father.

But as much as I espoused self-reliance, even I had to admit the disappearance of an entire people's only water source may not be something human hands could solve.

At her questioning look, I murmured, "That must be why I have been seeing so many tribeswomen here, as of late. They are seeking a sanctuary abundant with food and water."

"Yes," Nyra replied sadly. "It will not be long now until every oasis has dried up."

I startled, sure I had misheard. "*All* of the oases in the tribelands are drying up?"

"Every last one." The bitterness in her voice was reflected in her eyes. "The smallest ones, the lifewater of the Gorata and Akangli tribes were the first to evaporate. The Mamphele and Dineo were soon to follow. The largest oasis, controlled by the Buboloki Tribe, is now nearly spent."

"I had no idea it had gotten so bad, so quickly." I gazed at Nyra sympathetically. If I had been in her shoes, if it were Astoria's lakes that had run dry, what would I have done? In such a hopeless situation, could I have found a solution that did not rely on the magic of the stars?

Nyra squared her shoulders, a determined set to her jaw as she placed her free hand on top of mine. "That is why I have come—to save my people from sharing my sister's fate. Orion, will you help me petition the king to grant my wish?"

5

Astrid

"Astrid, I cannot thank you enough," Terry said as he enfolded my hands in his. The kind grandfather's eyes were bright with unshed tears. "My darling granddaughter has nearly made a full recovery."

"I am glad to hear it," I replied warmly. He seemed so much livelier, so full of life without fear for his family weighing him down. "The remedy you learned to make today should speed up her recovery, but please reach out to me should you or yours ever need help."

"I will." He patted my hands lovingly, and for a moment, I found myself wishing for a loving grandfather of my own. My life would have taken a far different course had my own grandfather cherished me, instead of chasing out me and my mother..

"Off I go then." He released my hands to carefully pick up the bottled remedy he had made today during class. This time, he had not needed much help, or a replacement remedy for that matter. "Oh, but what do you think those two whippersnappers are up to today?"

"Nova and Castor? I am not sure. Perhaps something came up," I mused slowly. Usually, those two were the ones to stay behind after class, instead of Terry. I had even waived their class fees for today—it was unlike them not to at least send word that they would be absent.

"Give them my thanks when you see them," Terry called as he shuffled slowly out the door. "They were such a help last week."

"I will." I returned his wave as he left, before turning my attention to tidying up.

"Why the long face?" Sirius asked as he stepped into the small room a few minutes later. His blonde hair was damp with sweat, but his eyes shone with vigor. He must have just finished up his own class, then.

With a start, I realized I had been scowling as I scrubbed at a particularly stubborn bit of crusted-on herb paste.

"Two of my regulars did not come to class today." I sighed, and handed over the cloth I had been using, gesturing at the paste. "Here, put those muscles to good use."

Sirius rolled his eyes, but obediently took the cloth and began scrubbing. "No need to take it personally, Astrid. Problems have a way of cropping up when we least expect them. I am sure they will come again when they can."

"Nova and Castor have never missed a class before, not without letting me know in advance. Both want to become apprentice herbalists when they come of age next year, and I had even waived their class fees for today." I folded my arms across my chest.

Sirius paused his scrubbing to look at me. "You fear something has happened to them."

I nodded. He went back to scrubbing.

"Do you know where they live?"

"At the crown-sponsored orphanage." I bit my lip.

"Why not check on them, then?" Sirius suggested. "Unless you had something else to do?"

"Just cleaning up here and making dinner for everyone." I glanced at the angle of the sun—sunset was not far off.

"I can finish up here and get dinner started. You go check on those future apprentices of yours," he offered.

"Thanks, Sirius. I appreciate it." After double-checking that my medicine bag was secure, I left the apothecary's back room and emerged onto the sunny streets.

As I was wending my way through housewives laden with supplies for dinner and husbands returning from a long day's work, my thoughts raced ahead of me to the orphanage. Surely, if some catastrophe had befallen them, or if some of the children had become ill, they would have reached out to the guild.

I always made time for my former home, no matter how busy I was. They usually called for me to treat cases of the sniffles here and there, or to splint a sprained ankle. Nova and Castor had always asked to watch, even back when I was simply experimenting with various remedies in my room. The pair had been fascinated by work, and excited by the prospect of learning how to help others feel better as well.

The low timbre of a voice I would know anywhere drew me from my thoughts, and I glanced around sharply. Orion was walking just a few yards in front of me. What perfect timing!

Just as I was about to call out to him, however, he turned, addressing the person beside him. My blossoming smile froze, before wilting on my lips. The soft expression on his face was one I rarely got the chance to see, and it was directed at a young tribeswoman. Her dark hair cascaded down her back, contrasting starkly against her red and yellow garments, as she turned her head to laugh at whatever Orion had said.

Orion was looking at *her* the way I had always hoped he would look at *me*.

I pressed my lips into a thin line, doing my best to squash the writhing feeling of jealousy that coiled like a serpent in the pit of my stomach. Was *she* the reason Orion had been paying fewer visits to the guild as of late? Why he had seemed oddly distracted? Regardless, I was on a mission—and I was taking him with me. I lifted my chin stubbornly and jogged forward, darting between people until I reached Orion.

"Orion!" I touched his arm lightly, and he looked over in surprise.

"Astrid! What a coincidence." At the look on my face, however, his easy grin faltered. He pulled me to the side, away from the flow of pedestrians. The tribeswoman followed close behind.

"Who is this, Orion?" she asked in a silky voice. I resisted the urge to wrinkle my sensitive nose at the faint scent of her too-sweet perfume.

"Nyra, this is Astrid. She is the best herbalist in the kingdom, and second-in-command of Hyperion. Astrid, Nyra." He hurried to make the introductions, but despite my placid expression, he could tell something was off.

"What a pleasure to meet one of Orion's people," Nyra said warmly. Her dark eyes glinted like chips of onyx in her oval-shaped face, unreadable.

"The pleasure is mine," I murmured politely with a carefully blank face, before turning back to Orion. "If you can spare the time, I need you to come with me."

His brows pinched together. "The situation is that dire?"

"I am uncertain," I confessed, but rushed on when his scowl deepened. "Nova and Castor missed class today. It may be nothing, but I am on my way to the orphanage. Orion, I have this horrible feeling..."

"Your intuition is rarely wrong," Orion murmured after a moment. "I really should go with her. But..." Orion hesitated as he turned to Nyra, as if he were reluctant to cut their time together short. "Would you like to tag along?"

"I would love to," Nyra purred, giving us both a smile.

I blinked, but showed no other outward surprise. Inside, though, I was taken aback. It was unlike Orion to be so trusting of a stranger, especially to the point of inviting her along. How much time, exactly, had he spent with this foreigner?

"This way, then." I merged back into the flow of traffic and walked briskly to the orphanage, which was located in a quiet part of town that I knew like the back of my hand. The pair had to hustle to keep up.

This orphanage in particular was funded by the crown, so the children were rarely in want of anything. It had been created as the result of someone's wish from many years ago, and was the perfect example of a wish that could be granted without the help of magic—and exactly the sort of wish Orion had no qualms about, unlike those that involved the magic of the stars.

Evelyn's Home was nestled in between a neighborhood and a park, and the building itself could comfortably house dozens of children at a time. Ivy climbed up the red brick facade and framed each window, giving it an air of dignified elegance. My old home looked exactly as I remembered it.

But as I approached, I heard no spritely laughter or running feet from within or without. An eerie quiet lay upon the building, and my knock on the front door went unanswered for quite some time.

I glanced back at Orion, his grim expression matching mine. This was not a good sign. I had never seen the place so...dead. My sense of foreboding mounted with every added moment of silence.

Finally, the assistant caretaker, Sally, cracked open the door. Her weary expression brightened when she spotted first me and then Orion. I noted her unkempt hair and the dark circles beneath her normally bright blue eyes with rising concern.

"Oh, Astrid and Orion! Am I glad to see you! I was just about to send someone to Hyperion." The relief in her voice was palpable. "Please, come in. Your...guest, as well."

"Sally, have the children taken ill? Where is Theo?" I questioned as she ushered us into the hall that still smelled like home.

"Castor fell ill a few days ago, and a few others followed suit. Theo went to purchase some remedies, but he has since fallen ill as well. At first, we thought the ailment was simply the spring sniffles, but the remedies had little effect," Sally explained sadly.

"Have dark bruises appeared on their skin?" I laid a hand on her thin shoulder. She seemed surprised and worried by my intensity.

"They appeared yesterday," Sally whispered, as if saying the words out loud made it too real. "Is it...?"

"The plague." Sally put a hand to her mouth, aghast. I felt like doing the same—I still had very little to show for my research into a cure. What rotten timing!

"Have you already reached out to the king for aid?" Orion asked.

"Yes, but we have yet to hear anything back. Which is...understandable, considering how many new cases must be cropping up," Sally said, looking down.

"That is still no excuse," Orion growled. I looked at him, surprised by the anger I heard in his voice.

"How terrible," Nyra murmured. "Surely the king will grant the wishes of these poor children, yes?"

Orion's expression tightened.

"I do not want to risk you catching the plague as well, Nyra. We will have to continue our conversation another time," Orion apologized, taking her hand in his. I tried not to bristle.

"I wish I could stay and help, but...I fear I have a poor bedside manner," Nyra replied with a self-deprecating laugh. And then, to my utter shock, she rose onto her toes and pressed a quick kiss to Orion's cheek. "I do hope to hear a favorable answer from you soon."

Before any of us could react, she nodded respectfully to me and Sally and saw herself out. Sally's eyebrows had shot towards her forehead, and Orion just stood there looking dazedly at the door.

"Sally, have the afflicted been isolated?" I asked after pointedly clearing my throat.

"Yes."

"Good, take us to them." Orion snapped out of it enough to follow as the assistant led us through the spacious home and to the east wing.

"The most severe cases are beyond this door," Sally said nervously. "A few others have the sniffles, but have responded well to the remedies, so they are on a different floor."

"Thank you, Sally. We shall take it from here," I told her gently, resting my hand on her arm for a moment.

She sagged in relief before hurrying away. I could hardly blame her for being fearful of catching the plague, especially since it was still so unclear how it was spreading. I supposed Orion and I were the odd ones, for putting ourselves at risk like this.

Orion opened the door to a pitiful scene. Four beds were pushed against the walls, three holding sick orphans, including poor Castor, and one holding Theo, the main caretaker of this place and the only father I had ever known. No wonder it had been so silent. The man's normally lively eyes were lined with fatigue and pain, and his tawny brown hair clung to his forehead. They all took turns coughing weakly, and I could see dark bruising creeping along their exposed skin.

"Orion!" Theo's eyes widened and he tried to sit up, only to have Orion gently push him back down.

"I am sorry to see you in this state, old friend." Even the sight of the blooming marks on Theo's skin was not enough to make Orion hesitate.

"You and me both." Theo's laugh quickly devolved into a wheezing cough. "Astrid, how good to see you! Perhaps, had I sent for you when Castor first fell ill, it would not have come to this."

I moved to his side, and took the hand he held out to me. Theo had always seemed so much larger than life, but now his big hand felt weak and frail in mine. I hated seeing him like this.

"Yes, you should have sent someone to the guild right away," I scolded gently. "You know I am never too busy for you and the others."

"I know, I know. It still feels like just yesterday you were holed up in your room upstairs, mixing together whatever herbs you could get your hands on into remedies to test on the rest us," he rasped, his warm brown eyes finding mine.

"Lucky for you I did," I retorted. And lucky for all of us that I had run into Orion on my way here. "I happen to have some remedies on hand. Orion, would you administer these to the children that just have a cold?"

"Of course," he rumbled. I could see how Theo's state was affecting the guildmaster too.

I appreciated how in times like this, Orion always allowed me to take the lead, and did his best to provide whatever support I needed. It was a strange reversal of our usual roles, but it was his faith in me and my abilities that had helped me more than anything else.

I gently removed my hand from Theo's so I could hand over a bundle of remedy vials to Orion. He cradled them as if they were liquid starlight, and I gave him a strained but grateful smile.

"I will see what I can do here, in the meantime." Then I moved closer to Orion, and lowered my voice to a whisper. "These four may need more help than I can give at this point, but I will still do what I can."

Orion nodded grimly in understanding. His clear blue eyes met mine, and I saw the same determination and kindness there that had made me want to follow him in the first place, that had drawn me to him from the start. He did not look particularly excited about the prospect of having to perform some of his "miracles," as usual, but I knew he could never turn his back on anyone here.

"Whatever it takes."

6

Orion

"Sally," I said when I spotted her hurrying through the carpeted halls, "Astrid gave me some remedies for the children with simple colds. Could you lead me to them?"

"Of course, right this way," she replied. "With Astrid's work, I am certain they will be well within the week. She has always been so talented." She gave me a relieved smile. "Nova's remedies have helped, but this has been a hard illness for them to shake."

"Hyperion would not be where it is today without her," I added. Beyond just her healing skills, Astrid was the glue that held the guild together, especially when I was away. Her help was invaluable.

"We are all glad to see her so happy whenever she visits." Sally glanced at me sidelong. "And I know you are a big part of that."

I looked down at the glass vials in my hands, the mint-colored liquid within sloshing with each step. Astrid had certainly come out of her shell since I first met her. But was Sally implying that...? No, surely not. I cared for Astrid, but I had never thought of her in *that* way before.

"How long has it been since you first contacted the crown?" I followed the assistant up a set of stairs to the second floor, studiously averting my eyes.

She pursed her lips, but said nothing about the abrupt change in subject. She frowned.

"Over a week," she finally answered.

Now it was my turn to scowl. What were those fools in the committees doing? Forget sending aid, they had not even acknowledged the request! In the past, they had generally seemed on top of things, but perhaps there were not enough members to handle an increase in health-related requests. If I could just convince my father to delegate more responsibilities to me... I would have to speak with him again, and request jurisdiction over the committees charged with maintaining past wishes.

I grimaced. Then again, if he granted my request and all of the problems were miraculously solved, I risked exposing my secret and losing my ability to help at all. It might be wiser to see if I could convince one of the committee members to send me information in a...less official capacity.

"Here we are," Sally said, pulling me from my thoughts. She opened a nondescript door to reveal a room full of children, all bedridden but in good spirits.

"Orion?" asked one sleepily.

"Orion is here!" cried another.

"It is good to see you little stars," I said warmly as I came in. "Though I am sorry it is under such circumstances."

"What did you bring us?"

"These are remedies for those red noses of yours." I laughed at the faces some of them made when they heard that. "Astrid made them herself."

"Astrid came too?" the child brightened.

"She is with Theo and the others right now, helping them get better too." To Sally, I asked, "Would you help me administer these?"

"Of course," she murmured, and I dutifully handed over half of the vials.

I approached the closest child and sat on the edge of his bed. I put the other vials in my lap and uncorked one, which I helped the little boy to drink. He wrinkled his nose in distaste.

"Tastes too minty," he complained.

"Still better than the charcoal flavor of the ones the regular apothecaries have you take, right Ren?" I gave him a pat on the back.

"I suppose. At least Astrid *tries* to make them taste better," he admitted.

"Even when the taste is still a tad off the mark," I finished the unspoken part of that sentence. Ren grinned, and I grinned back. "Be grateful you are not the one who gets to test out the new flavors."

Ren's eyes went wide as I laughed, and I gathered up the other vials and ruffled his hair affectionately before I moved on to the next patient. Sally did the same along the other side of the room, and most of the children drank the remedies with only a little cajoling from us. They all knew Astrid would always do right by them.

Finally, I got to the last bed in my row, which held a girl Astrid had affectionately nicknamed Nova, for her fiery spirit. If I remembered correctly, she had just turned fourteen, and was hoping to follow in Astrid's footsteps when she came of age next year. She looked more exhausted than the others, with her ruby red hair hanging limply around her pale face.

"Your turn, Nova," I handed her an uncorked vial, and she drank it down without hesitation.

"How is Castor?" she croaked, and I could hear the fear in her voice. Unlike the younger ones, she likely suspected the gravity of the situation.

"Astrid is tending to him now. He will be fine, Nova." Neither I nor Astrid would be leaving until they were all out of mortal danger.

"But if he really does have the...the plague..." her voice dropped to a whisper, and she fisted the sheets in her thin hands.

Nearby heads turned in curiosity at the sudden change in pitch, and I sighed. This was not a conversation to have near the little ones.

"Nova, how would you like to help me carry the empty vials down to Astrid? I think Sally can manage up here for a time." I looked to the assistant for confirmation, which she gave.

Nova's eyes lit up, and she immediately got out of bed. She wobbled as she stood, but brushed off my attempts to assist her. She was a determined one, I would give her that. She moved from bed to bed and collected each vial, using the bottom of her tunic as a pouch to carry them all.

We left Sally with the children and began walking down the stairs, back towards the room with the worst cases. It was a risk bringing Nova with me, but I had a sneaking suspicion that she had been paying her closest friend visits already.

"I wish I were as talented as Astrid," Nova said sadly, without looking at me. "Then I could have helped everyone, before it came to this. And I would not have had to find help from others."

"You and Castor are still learning. No one expects you to take on that kind of responsibility just yet," I tried to console her. "None of this is your fault, Nova."

"But by the time Astrid was my age, she was already practicing as a full-fledged herbalist for Hyperion. And helping all kinds of people," she protested as we descended the stairs.

"You two are quite alike, in that regard." Nova finally looked at me. "Just like you, Astrid was always eager to keep learning, so she could help the people who needed her. She worked hard, and now we have all come to rely on her. But in the beginning, she still struggled a good deal with creating effective remedies. It took much trial and error before she got it right."

"*Astrid* had a hard time making remedies?" Nova asked in disbelief.

"She did. She started out much like you and Castor, learning from others and trying her best to improve on existing remedies." I glanced at her from the corner of my eye, happy to see her expression had lightened.

"Theo and Sally never mentioned that part," she murmured.

"Sally did tell me earlier how your remedies have been helping everyone a great deal over the last week," I added for good measure.

"Truly?" Some of the sparkle had come back to her tired eyes.

"Truly. Once you are both well, perhaps you could come by the guild and assist Astrid with her workload. I will have to ask her first, of course, but you two might be able to offer her a new perspective, and even just having two extra sets of hands to help with her usual work could free her to spend more time on developing new remedies."

"I would love to learn from her, beyond her weekly classes! And I know Castor would, too." Nova smiled to herself, her mood considerably improved just as we reached the room.

I opened the door, and Nova greeted Astrid warmly as she carefully deposited the vials where Astrid indicated. Then she rushed right over to Castor, her smile evaporating when she saw the state he was in. The sun was just beginning to set, casting beams of golden light through the windows, making the patients appear even more pale and sickly by comparison. It looked like Theo and the others had fallen asleep, likely thanks to one of Astrid's remedies, but putting the teenager to sleep would be too risky at this point.

Castor looked to be in dire straits. He did not have the strength to sit up, and his shallow breathing gave way to coughing fits every few minutes. While Nova tried to cheer him up, Astrid drew me back to the door, and I could tell from the look on her face how serious this was.

"How are the little ones upstairs?" she asked without preamble.

"They all took your remedy, and I am sure they will be well soon. Ren already looks to be on the mend," I dutifully reported. She seemed relieved.

"Good, good." But then she glanced back at the four patients worriedly.

"How long do they have?" I asked quietly.

"For Theo and the two others? A few days, at most. For Castor?" She shook her head. "I tried giving them all a few drops of liquified starlight, which seemed to help stabilize them for a time, but..."

"Could they have caught it in town?" I murmured.

"Hard to say. This sickness is bizarre—it is not progressing the way a normal sickness would." She bit her lip. "It is almost as if their bodies are simply shutting down." Astrid's gaze fell upon the two teenagers.

The setting sun silhouetted Nova and Castor, casting their faces in deep shadow. Soon, the skies would darken, allowing the stars to shine. Just in time to boost the amulet's power.

I let out a breath, resigning myself to what I knew would come next.

"Beyond dulling their pain, there is nothing more I can do for them," Astrid whispered as she turned back towards me. "But Castor will not survive the night. Your miracles are the only thing that can save him now."

"What...?" rasped a voice from behind Astrid. "What do you mean he...he will not... But you said you could help him!"

Astrid turned in surprise to see that Nova had snuck up behind us unnoticed. The blood had drained from her face, her already drawn features turning as white as a sheet. I reached out a hand to comfort her, but she flinched away.

"Nova—" Astrid started.

"No!" Nova cut her off. "No! You have to help him! You have to save him! Please, I...I am begging you! There has to be something, anything you can do!"

Nova gripped Astrid's skirts tightly as she slid to the floor. Tears gathered in her eyes and dripped down her sallow cheeks. Astrid looked at me helplessly, at a loss for what to say.

"Nova," I said as I crouched down in front of her, "Do you trust me and Astrid?"

"Yes," she sniffled

"Castor and the other three will be well by morning. I guarantee it." I held her pained gaze without wavering. I would not let her, or any of them, down. Even if I hated the magic I would have to use to save them.

Whatever she found in my eyes seemed to reassure her, and she finally nodded, though she kept ahold of Astrid. I glanced at the window, relieved to see that twilight was finally descending.

Hopefully, the starlight seeping through the window would be enough to bolster the amulet's power.

"Astrid, would you help Nova back up to her bed?" I requested. For a moment, I thought I saw a whisper of sadness in her eyes, but she blinked and it was gone.

"Yes. I will be waiting, whenever you are done." Astrid helped the girl to stand, and shepherded her out the door, despite Nova's weak protests.

Once their footsteps had faded, I rose to close and lock the door behind them. Next, I went to each window and opened the shutters, just as the first stars began to appear in the velvety sky. I angled them in such a way that the starlight beamed down, but no one on the street would be able to see in. Then, I took a spare rag and stuffed it into the crack beneath the door. Since we were not in the guild, I had to take extra precautions.

My gaze swept the room, and once I was satisfied that no one could see in, I moved to Castor's bed and sat on the edge. He watched me silently, but there was no fear in his steely gray eyes.

"I never thought I would get to learn the secret of your miracles," Castor rasped, but then was hit with a coughing fit. Once it had passed, he added, "Nova is going to be so jealous."

"That she will," I said with a chuckle, but sobered quickly. "Can you promise never to speak of what transpires in this room, to anyone? My ability to continue helping people depends on your silence."

"I vow on the stars above that I will never share your secrets," Castor promised solemnly.

"Thank you, Castor." I gave him a brief smile. "Now, I need you to listen very carefully. You are going to make a wish for yourself, Theo, Thomas and Jonathon to be completely healthy, now and forevermore. The wording must be exactly right."

"So that is how you do it," Castor whispered, his eyes widening in awe. But then he frowned. "Can I not wish for everyone to be healthy?"

"If only it were that simple." I smiled sadly. "If you wished for everyone to be healthy, that could be interpreted as every living creature in the world. Even if I used all of the starlight in the sky and added the entirety of my own lifeforce on top of it, I could not grant such a wish."

"You would die?" Castor looked horrified.

"Most likely. Even having your wish include three others is pushing it." I ran a hand through my hair, grimacing.

"I never knew there was a cost to granting wishes," Castor said with a weak cough. "Wait, would saving the four of us cost you some of your life? Then I refuse to make the wish!"

His declaration restored a sliver of my faith in humanity.

"I have enough starlight stored up in my amulet, so the cost to me should be minimal, if anything. But I appreciate your concern." I put a hand on his too-thin shoulder as my heart warmed, and withdrew the amulet from beneath my tunic. "Make your wish, Castor."

The teenager looked between me and the small part of the star sapphire that he could see through my fingers, before he finally nodded and closed his eyes.

"I wish for myself, Theo, Thomas and Jonathon, the ones in this room, to be made completely healthy, now and forevermore."

I closed my eyes and gripped the amulet tighter as I drew forth its magic. Shimmering silver starlight poured from the amulet, moving on a phantom breeze to encircle each of the individuals named in the wish. More and more starlight filled the room, joined by the light coming through the shutters. The light beyond my closed eyelids grew in brilliance until it was nearly unbearable.

I felt a tug on the core of my being as the amulet reached for more power, so I swiftly released Castor's shoulder and retrieved the spare bottle of starlight I always kept in my pocket for emergencies. I popped off the cork and upended the bottle over the amulet, which greedily drank it in. The tug on my soul eased, and then vanished entirely. I sighed with relief, and focused on guiding the mounting magic to fulfill its purpose.

The starlight flared brightly before it sank into each of the four people. As it burned away the plague and strengthened them against it and anything like it, I felt four points of intense pain in my back. I gritted my teeth against the fire in my skin, knowing that when the pain faded, there would be four new stars engraved in my back.

For the first time in recent memory, I did not feel the stirrings of resentment towards the magic that had taken my mother from me. How could I, when a few minutes of pain ensured my little friend's survival?

7

Astrid

"All better, Nova—oof." Nova interrupted Castor as she tackled him in a hug. I noticed her arms were shaking with relief.

"Never do that to me again," Nova whisper-yelled, with tears in her eyes. "You are not allowed to leave me alone again."

"I...I promise I am not going anywhere." The boy's eyes misted over.

Castor wrapped his arms around her, and laid his head on top of hers. She clung onto him like she never wanted to let go, like he was the most precious thing in the world to her.

I imagine I had behaved much the same when Orion rescued me from that slaver, Khalifon.

Orion smiled tiredly from where he leaned against the doorframe, his arm just barely brushing mine. After he had emerged from the room, I had checked on each of the four patients, three of whom were still asleep, and was incredibly relieved to find they were well. The dark bruising had vanished completely from their skin, and their breathing had all eased. They looked as if they had never even been ill at all, let alone at death's doorstep.

I found myself wondering once more what Orion's miracles truly were. They must be some kind of magic, for no remedy could possibly work so quickly or have such universal success, even one brewed by a druid. I glanced at him askance. Was it possible he hailed from one of the magical races beyond Astoria's borders, as I did?

"Thank the stars." Nova drew back just far enough to look Castor over. Stark relief shone on her face when she saw all the pale skin where the bruising had once been.

"Thank Orion—he saved me. He saved all of us." Castor grinned at him over the top of Nova's head.

"Thank you so much, Orion!" Nova came and threw her arms around him next. I smiled to myself.

Orion stiffened for a moment, as if in pain, but swiftly swept the girl up into his arms and twirled her around, before setting her carefully back on her feet. My brows pinched together as I closely watched my guildmaster's face. I had seen enough patients to be able to tell when one was hiding his pain.

What did his miracles require of him, that a hug would hurt?

"You are most welcome." He patted Nova's back comfortingly.

"How did you do it? Was it a special potion? Even the tribesman I talked to said his cure contained expensive ingredients and took ages to make." Nova was looking at Orion with unadulterated admiration on her face.

I stepped forward, curiosity and excitement flickering to life like a candle. "Nova, you spoke with someone who has created a cure for the plague?"

"He showed it to me. Of course, he refused to tell me what was in it, beyond that it was a mixture of medicinal herbs from the Talahari Desertlands."

I exchanged a glance with Orion, and saw that he was just as excited as I was. What if the refugees had accidentally brought this plague with them? If it came from the tribes, then it would make sense they would also know how to treat it. The thought had simply never occurred to me.

"Was it effective?" Orion asked.

Nova shook her head. "I never got the chance to find out. I was going to meet with him tomorrow afternoon, once I had gathered enough gold to pay for it."

I frowned. "How much was he asking for his cure?" Not that Nova could have even administered it in time to save Castor.

"F-Five gold," she stammered.

"Five gold! A family of four could survive on that for two years!" I exclaimed, taken aback. If the cure was truly that costly to make, it would be difficult for Hyperion to produce enough to meet the need, if it continued spreading like this. Alarm bells rang in my head, but I was careful not to let my suspicions show on my face.

Orion folded his arms across his chest. "I suppose you intended to give him the orphanage's funding, which was why you planned to meet him tomorrow."

Nova nodded mutely. Castor put a comforting arm around her shoulders. "At least I no longer need it." She leaned her head against Castor's.

"I want you to take us to him tomorrow." Orion looked at me in surprise, but then slowly nodded as understanding dawned in his eyes. "If he truly has a cure for the plague, then we can ask for the recipe. If he refuses to sell it, we can always buy the cure and I can attempt to recreate it myself."

"That is a marvelous idea." Orion looked so relieved that I wondered again what his miracles cost him. "Will you do that for us?"

"Anything for you," Nova said without hesitation. Castor nodded.

"Thank you," Orion said, and the two teenagers beamed.

"But in the future, come to me and Astrid—or anyone in Hyperion, for that matter—first, before the crown, or some tribesman on the street. Regardless of what the problem is, whether someone has the sniffles or funds are tight, I want you to let us know right away." He leveled his gaze on them, to convey the gravity of his words.

"Of course, but..." Nova said slowly, "How will we contact you?"

I glanced at Orion, and he raised an eyebrow at me. It was up to me, then.

"If Orion approves, I was thinking of having both of you work at the guild a few days a week as my apprentices, since you are both nearly of age anyways. You could help me with my classes and regular workload, and perhaps even assist me with formulating new remedies. As guild members, you would both receive your own starsteel watches as well." I glanced at Orion, whose eyebrows had begun inching towards his dark hair. Normally he was the one to invite new members, and he always had final say.

"Not just apprentices, but new members, eh?" he commented drily, eyeing the pair with renewed scrutiny.

"Oh please, Orion?" Castor asked eagerly.

"We promise not to get in the way! We will do whatever you say! It would be a dream come true to be Astrid's apprentices!" Nova was bouncing on the balls of her feet in excitement.

"Hmm," Orion said, tilting his head to one side as he considered. "Astrid *has* been increasingly busy as of late. I suppose she *could* use a couple extra pairs of hands. But on one condition."

"Anything!" Nova replied immediately.

Orion eyed the pair, who were both holding their breaths and watching him with wide eyes. When his gaze softened, I had the feeling that I would have a couple of eager ducklings following me around for the next few years.

"You must follow her instructions exactly, and promise to keep her recipes a secret."

"That was two conditions," Castor said with a laugh.

Orion raised a single eyebrow.

"But we will happily agree to both, right Castor?" Nova quickly said, and elbowed the boy in the ribs.

"Right, of course," he gasped, rubbing his side.

"You start as soon as Nova is fully well," I said with a satisfied smile.

Now it was my turn to be tackled by an incredibly excited Nova. I laughed, and rubbed the younger girl's back.

"I promise we will not let you down!" Nova exclaimed.

"Welcome to the family." Orion extended a hand to Castor, and the boy shook it, something akin to awe and love shining in his eyes. "Hyperion will be expecting great things from the both of you."

"I will do my best to live up to that." The boy was grinning from ear to ear.

"Orion and I will come again tomorrow, so we can meet this tribesman-herbalist. But for now, you two need to get some rest. There will be no idle hands in my workshop." My tone was firm, but I kept my expression warm.

"Fine," Nova grumbled. "Goodnight. And...Orion?"

"Yes?"

"Thank you for keeping your promise." Nova flashed him a shy smile before she bounded out of the room, presumably back to her bed.

"You have your work cut out for you with that one," Orion said to Castor. I chuckled.

"I would not have her any other way." He grinned.

"Good answer." Orion clapped him on the back and followed me out of the room, after I blew out the candle and plunged the room into restful darkness.

We ran into Sally on the way to the door, and informed her that the four were out of danger, and that everyone would be recovered within a few days. She slumped in relief, and I could see how heavy a toll her worries and responsibilities had taken.

"You did well, Sally," I reassured her. "Without you, things would have been much worse. You can rest easy now."

"I do not know how to thank you both," she said tearfully.

"Please let us know right away next time if anything like this ever happens again," Orion requested solemnly. I always appreciated how considerate he was of everyone in my former home.

"I will."

"We will return tomorrow to check on everyone." I smiled at the woman who had helped raise me, hating that I was keeping news of a potential cure from her. But I wanted to spare her the pain of having her hopes raised, only to be dashed, if this cure proved to be a fake.

We said our goodbyes and began the walk back to the guild house. I glanced up at the star-filled sky, and gave a silent prayer of thanks for the blessing of their starlight. Without this kingdom and the people in it, I never would have lived to see this day.

I glanced at Orion beside me as he breathed out a sigh of relief, and watched the cloud of his breath as it puffed white in the crisp night air. He seemed relieved to be back outside of that stuffy room and beneath the stars. I shivered as the night breeze nipped at my bare arms, and found myself blushing when Orion removed his coat and draped it around my shoulders. His warmth still lingered in the thick fabric, and his scent of cedarwood teased my nose.

"Thank you," I murmured. I clutched his coat around my shoulders with one slim hand, my own breath pluming in the air and mingling with his.

"Thank you for going to check on them today," Orion said grimly. "I do not even want to consider what might have happened if you had not."

"It was a good thing I ran into you on the way," I replied, just as seriously. I tried to ignore the fact that he had not been alone. "There was little I could do for those four on my own."

"Is a cure even possible? I...I only have so many miracles in me, Astrid." His worry and exhaustion leached into his tone, and I brushed my shoulder against his comfortingly. I knew he would never voice his doubts in front of the others, and it warmed me from the inside out that he trusted me with this, if not his secrets.

"There has to be. Even if the tribesman tomorrow is nothing but a con artist, I promise you I will do everything I can to find a cure." It seemed even Orion's miracles had their limits.

"I have faith in you. Coin is not a problem—spare no expense on research. Whatever it takes," he said. "Hopefully, Castor and Nova could take over some of your regular work to free up your time for work on a cure."

"I had a feeling that was what you had in mind when you suggested it," I responded. "I have no doubt they will both be a great help."

We walked in silence for a time, each of us lost in our own thoughts. Normally, walking alone at night was something I avoided, but I felt safe by Orion's side. The starsteel sword at his hip and his muscular frame would make any late-night opportunists think twice before bothering us.

The lampposts glowed steadily, their pools of light like stars on earth. For some reason, instead of tomorrow's all-important meeting to buy the cure, my mind kept circling back to that tribeswoman and the way she had pecked Orion's cheek. As long as I had known him, Orion had never so much as mentioned seeing anyone.

"What did Nyra mean?" I suddenly asked into the quiet. "About waiting for a favorable response?"

"Oh, that," Orion sighed, rubbing a hand against the back of his neck. "Nyra asked for my help petitioning the king to grant her wish to restore the dried-up oases in the desert."

"What?!" I stumbled on an uneven cobblestone. Orion's arm shot out and steadied me. "But that sort of geographic alteration is beyond even the power of the stars! Even if it were not... Orion, helping her goes against everything you stand for, everything you believe in!"

"I told her it was likely impossible, and even if it were not, that the king is duty-bound to grant the wishes of his own subjects before those of a foreigner." He grimaced. "But she still wants to try."

"Why you? Why does it have to be you?" I tried not to let my emotions seep into my voice.

"Since I am both a native-born Astorian and a guildmaster, she believes I have the most knowledge of how to go about guiding her through the process. Which I do, to be fair."

"But Hyperion's main goal is to empower people to rely on *themselves*, instead of the king's wishes. If you help her get her wish granted, everyone else will want the same!" Was Orion that enamored with this tribeswoman, that he would throw away everything he had built for her? My stomach soured at the possibility, and I tugged his coat tighter around me.

"I know." Orion pinched the bridge of his nose. "You are right, Astrid. The odds of success are so slim that it is laughable. Tomorrow, I should just gently turn her down, and recommend that she do some research on well-digging or seek a new place to live."

My sense of victory that he had sided with me and his own ideals was short-lived, washed away by a lingering sense of guilt. I was sympathetic to Nyra's plight, even if I wished she had asked someone else for assistance.

I looked away, up to the distant stars that I could never repay. Orion was not the only one with secrets, and one of mine was the fact that although I generally agreed with his philosophy, I could never support the complete removal of wish-granting.

Because there were some problems only wishes could solve. And I would not even be alive were it not for the wish my mother had made, and been granted.

8

Orion

"Focus, Your Highness!" Rigel grunted as he shifted his wooden practice blade, so it glanced off my shoulder instead of my neck. "What has you so distracted these days?"

"Nothing in particular." The knight easily parried my thrust, and the subsequent strikes. I wiped the sweat from my brow.

He was right, though—I had been finding it difficult to concentrate, lately. And it certainly did not help that I had been granting more wishes than usual at the guild lately. I was exhausted, but there was no end in sight, considering how many more plague victims were discovered every day.

I did not even want to think about what I would do when it came time for the quarterly wish festival, when I would have to relinquish the amulet. I would just have to cross that bridge when I came to it. Hopefully by then, Astrid would have something resembling a cure.

Last night at the orphanage, Astrid had seemed rather...on edge. Lately, she had seemed increasingly bothered by my secrecy, but as much as I relied her, I was still afraid to tell her the truth. To see the sense of betrayal in her eyes when she learned who I was, that I had been lying to her for so many years.

Would she still treat me the same if she knew?

"Honestly, Prince Sterling." Rigel whacked my upper arm with the flat of his blade. "If you will not take this seriously, then there is little point to the exercise."

"Apologies, Sir Rigel. I have...much on my mind, as of late." I shoved any errant thoughts to the back of my mind, focusing entirely on the rough scrape of wood against my palm, the position of my feet and the angle of my sword.

"Perhaps talking about your concerns might lessen the burden." The swordsman struck, and nodded approvingly when I parried the blow properly this time.

"Oh? Are you willing to listen to my woes with women?" Dark, alluring eyes rose unbidden in my mind.

"W-what? *Women?*" The knight's sword lowered as his grip slackened with surprise.

I took advantage of that split-second when he let his guard down, striking with my sword. The thunk of wood hitting wood cracked into the early morning air, and a moment later the tip of my blade was hurtling towards my opponent's throat.

At the very last moment, Rigel brought his guard up, and my wooden sword bounced harmlessly to the side. Using that momentum, I swung around in an arc towards his now unguarded ribs. He danced to the side, my blade whooshing through empty air.

"Better," he grunted. "No wonder you have been wearing such a drawn expression. The womenfolk can certainly be mysterious creatures."

"That they can." I parried his next thrust, and dodged the follow-up strike. "Whether I win or lose the argument, I somehow wind up in the same amount of trouble."

"That explains why you have been disappearing off to town so frequently—it was to visit a lady friend!" The knight laughed, even as he expertly parried my blows.

"Something like that," I hedged. "So, Sir Rigel, if you found yourself disagreeing with your lady friend about matters of, say, policies and politics, would you continue arguing with her, or hold your tongue for the sake of peace?"

"I would hold my tongue, so long as we agreed on the subject of children, worship, and finances." The knight lunged forward, and I barely avoided the attack. "But in your case, I would say that depends on whether she knows of your...position."

"She does not. But I understand your concern." Our wooden blades thunked against one another.

"If she is not trying to influence a prince, then perhaps you could afford to hold your tongue, if doing so does not cause you anguish." Rigel unleashed a flurry of strikes, each landing on my blade with quick succession.

"That right there is the problem." I returned his strikes, matching blow for blow. "What kind of prince would I be if I did?"

The knight looked up at my words, a hint of something like awe in his steely eyes. I took the opportunity he unknowingly presented me and knocked his sword to the side, bringing the tip to hover before his heart.

Rigel smiled. "A good match, Your Highness."

"Only because you went easy on me." I smiled and lowered my practice sword, planting it in the dusty ground.

"Only in the beginning, Highness."

"Any progress on your investigations into the disappearance of those children?" I tried to keep my tone level, but I was sure he saw right through me. Rigel and his father were two of the only people who knew why I had such an interest in this particular issue.

"Not much, unfortunately. After what happened to you, most every slave trader was rounded up, thrown in the dungeons and made an example of, which kept any other opportunistic miscreants from trying their hand at it. It seems that lesson may have been forgotten ten-odd years later." Rigel scowled, and I shared in his frustration.

"If you catch wind of their base of operations, please inform me so that I may accompany the knights sent to capture them." I flipped my practice sword around in my hand, imagining what

I would do with a real one to those who dared to lay a hand on a child. Were that slave-trading bastard, Khalifon, still alive, I would happily drive it through his black heart.

"Of course, Highness. It always boosts the mens' morale when you join us on a raid. Rest assured, I will do whatever it takes to prevent another child from being condemned to a life in Harland's salt mines." The knight placed a calloused hand on my shoulder. "I have my best men working on it."

I dipped my head, glad to hear how seriously he was taking this problem. I never wanted anyone else to go through what Astrid and I did.

"Congratulations on your recent promotion to Knight Commander, by the way. It is well-earned, and I know your father must be proud." I tried to lighten the mood, and grinned at the answering pride on the knight's face.

"You honor me, Prince Sterling. I am truly grateful—the timing could not have been better." He bowed his head respectfully, then barked out a laugh. "But my old man will keel over before he acknowledges my hard work, though."

"You and me both, brother. Your father is an even tougher taskmaster than mine—perhaps that is why he can stand being the king's personal knight." I let out a chuckle of my own as I clapped the him on the back. Motion caught my eye, and I turned to see my attendant, Zale, hurrying towards me. "It would seem I am needed elsewhere. Until next time, Sir Rigel."

"Have fun with your lady friend, Highness." The knight winked at me, and I felt my ears grow warm.

I tossed him my wooden sword, and he bowed again as I headed for Zale. I drew alongside him, and he fell into step beside me. I glanced down at the papers he had clutched in his hands, most of which appeared to be documents for me to sign. I resisted the urge to sigh. I had asked for more responsibility, and here it was. My chance to prove myself to my father.

"What brings you to the land of 'dust and doofuses'?" I asked with a smirk. Zale was a man more suited to shuffling papers than swinging a sword, and made no secret of his disdain for the practice.

"A message from the king has just arrived for you." Zale produced an envelope sealed with blue wax and imprinted with my father's personal seal. "I thought it better not to wait, even if I had to brave the dustlands."

I snorted as I watched the man pick imaginary dust from his immaculate tunic. It was a good thing he was so diligent as an attendant—I could not picture him succeeding in more common, labor-intensive roles.

I broke the seal and unfolded the letter, pausing by an archway to scan the few lines it contained. I folded it neatly and stuffed it back into the envelope, and I could tell how curious my attendant was about the contents by the way he was fidgeting.

I would have to manage my time wisely today, but I could still fit everything in. That is, so long as my meeting with that tribesman did not run too long this afternoon.

"What did it say?" Zale finally asked.

I toyed with the idea of leaving him in suspense for a while, but I had a feeling he would retaliate with an increased workload for the day if I did. Better not to risk it.

"The king has requested my presence for dinner this evening," I finally relented.

"I would recommend bathing beforehand," Zale quipped, wrinkling his nose at me.

"How kind of you to offer to help me with the paperwork whilst I do so." I resumed walking, leaving Zale sputtering indignantly in my wake.

"I said no such thing!"

I just laughed.

A short time later, I took a deep breath as I left the towering gates of the castle behind me, and made my way into town. The streets were always bustling in the mid-afternoon, so it was far easier for me to blend in with the crowd.

I strolled along the cobblestones, taking a moment to get a sense of the general mood. Not too long ago, an errant cough would elicit little response from others, but now, people nearby would shy away from the source of the noise like startled deer. There was a tension in the air that revealed how the plague—and fear of it—had spread.

Thanks to the incident at the orphanage, I had learned that nearly every committee was being overwhelmed by an influx of requests for aid and wishes. The cause came as no surprise to me, though it had clearly taken my father's people off-guard. I had loaned Zale to them, so he could help with paperwork while they desperately hired new people.

But would it be enough? With only one amulet, and one person who was permitted to use it…

I had nearly gotten caught returning the amulet to its pedestal last night, when my father had been on his way to retrieve it for some emergency wish-granting. He had even mentioned to me his worries that the star sapphire was losing its magic.

How long did I have left before he began to suspect the true reason?

I sighed and pulled out my pocket watch and glanced at the time. Since Nova's scheduled meeting was not for another hour, I had some time to myself for research. I had no intention of going into this meeting blind—I wanted to gather as much information as possible beforehand.

And so I turned my steps down a familiar path, to the best place in town for rumor-gathering. Ace was exactly where I expected when I walked into his tavern: standing behind the bar, polishing a glass.

"What brings you in so early, Orion?" Ace greeted me. I chuckled good-naturedly as I approached the bar.

"Business, unfortunately. I wanted to ask—have you heard any rumors of tribesmen selling miraculous cures for the plague as of late?" I kept my voice lowered, even though there was hardly anyone in the tavern at this hour of the afternoon.

"Now that you mention it, I do recall hearing something to that effect over the last few days." Ace absently polished a glass as he spoke, sobering.

"Did any of them know if it was effective?" I leaned forward eagerly. It seemed a desperate teenager was not the only one with whom this tribesman had made contact.

"Not as far as I know. It sounded as if none of my patrons had the coin to purchase one just yet."

"How much for a vial?" If the tribesman had a limited quantity, then I would not be surprised to hear of him auctioning it off to the highest bidder.

"Hmmm. I heard anywhere from three gold to ten. Far more than most of my regulars earn in a year." Ace shook his head sadly.

I raised my eyebrows. "How greedy."

Ace grunted in agreement, but then frowned, as if something had occurred to him. "Why the sudden interest?"

"One of Astrid's students from the orphanage met this man, but did not have the coin to purchase his cure on the spot. I simply wanted to gather more information before I meet him this afternoon. It is my hope to buy the recipe from him so that Astrid can replicate it," I elaborated.

"Let me know when it is ready—I would be glad to send patients your way," Ace offered.

"Will do." Without looking, I pushed back from the counter, and felt my starsteel scabbard hit something behind me.

"Ouch."

"My apologies..." I trailed off, staring in confusion at the person I had bumped into. I could have sworn that was Nyra's voice, but the person in front of me looked like a common maiden, with mousy-brown hair and forgettable features. Except the edges of her silhouette seemed...blurry, somehow. I resisted the urge to rub my eyes.

"Thank you," she said, averting her eyes. I frowned. That was definitely Nyra's voice. I grabbed her arm, stepping closer.

"Nyra?" I gasped in confusion. The moment I had touched her, the girl's form had shivered, distorting, before fading away like mist. Now Nyra stood in front of me, her dark eyes wide with surprise.

She scowled down at the starsteel ring on my finger and let out a sigh. "Hello Orion."

"What...was that? Magic?" My eyes roved over her brightly-colored form in amazement.

"My people's mirage magic." She looked down pointedly at where I still gripped her bare wrist, and I hastily released her. My starsteel ring must have shattered the illusion.

I remembered reading about it in a history book, but I had not realized how completely convincing the illusion could be. It had been my understanding that mirage magic was a rare gift. "Can most people from the tribes wield this magic? And why were you using it in the first place?"

"Sometimes, it is a relief to not be given dirty looks wherever I go," she said a tad defensively. I winced. "Mirage magic is quite common. Young children practice by playing pranks on each other all the time."

"I understand." I had created my alter-ego for similar reasons. But then I fell silent, the air charged with things unsaid. I still had yet to give Nyra an answer on whether I would help her petition the king. I intended to turn her down, but had yet to find the right moment.

"What do you know of my people's magic?" Nyra suddenly asked.

"Not much beyond the fact that it is called mirage magic, and creates illusions."

"While that is true, it hardly scrapes the surface. The magic is in the application." Nyra winked at me. "Though I can only replicate what I have seen myself."

She pulled me aside, into a darker corner of the tavern, just as light began to bend and distort around her, the way I had seen the air shiver above stones baked by the sun. In the time it took me to blink, Nyra had completely transformed...into me. From my height and short, dark hair to the clothes I was wearing, every detail was there. Though I did notice a few spots that were blurry, like around my coat pockets and fingernails.

"That is...rather unnerving."

Nyra grinned back at me with my face. "Children often like to play pranks on each other by pretending to be someone else. Harmless games."

"Your voice is still yours, though," I noted. I stepped forward and waved my ring-free hand through my—her—hair. My fingers found only empty air, and the image rippled like the surface of a still pond when disturbed. The effect only ended a few moments after I had returned my hand to my side.

It felt like a barrel of ice water had been dumped over my head as the implications of her ability hit home. Nyra was right—it was all about the application. If the tribespeople had the ability to look like anyone of their choosing, then we were defenseless against them if they chose to infiltrate the castle or cause general havoc. Our soldiers would be unable to tell friend from foe on sight, without further investigation.

And even if she did not know it, she could waltz right into the castle while looking like me.

A light went on in my head. *This* must be how so many of Nyra's people were slipping across our borders, and making their way into Astoria. But what of the reports of the ones that were turned away? Were only a select few able to wield mirage magic, despite Nyra's assurances?

Or were they simply refusing to use it, to lull us into a false sense of security?

"Our magic can only manipulate light, not sound." She paused. "But your starsteel sword and ring disrupted the illusion."

I nodded mutely, jolted from my dire thoughts. I held out the hand that bore the starsteel ring as I stepped closer. The illusion began to ripple when I was three steps away, and wavered at one step. However, it only melted away completely once I had touched the metal to her bare skin. I pulled it back, and the illusion resumed. I set it against her clothes, and the magic fractured, like a broken mirror.

"Hmm. So only direct contact with skin completely breaks the illusion," I mused. That was an important distinction.

"It would seem so." She looked thoughtful. "The sensation is...rather unpleasant."

"I can imagine." The thought of being cut off from the starlight while I was granting a wish made my skin crawl.

Her dark eyes cut to mine, and I realized my mistake.

"If I was suddenly unable to use my hand, I doubt I would find the experience enjoyable, either," I hurried to say.

Her eyes softened and she nodded. I breathed an internal sigh of relief.

"Are skills or knowledge copied along with the appearance?" If the answer was yes, would she tell me?

"No, unfortunately," she said with a laugh. "If that were the case, it would be wonderfully helpful—I could simply copy an artisan or dancer's appearance, and never have to spend time practicing again!"

"Very true. Do you...use your magic often?" I asked, trying to sound nonchalant. Since I had yet to hear of any incidents involving mirage magic, I assumed the answer was no.

But then again, would most people even know the difference, or comprehend what they were seeing if they spotted a tribeswoman suddenly turn into an Astorian? Or would they brush it off as a trick of the light?

"No. As I said, it is mostly used by children to play pranks." Was I imagining it, or was there an edge to her voice? Perhaps talking about her homeland was too painful for her right now.

"Well, I am sure those children are rarely ever bored." I plastered a smile on my face, hoping to lighten the mood. I put my worries aside to focus on the present moment.

But instead, her eyes took on a stormy cast, and she looked down. "Yes, boredom is a foreign concept to them."

I placed my hand at the small of her back, and began to gently guide her outside, onto the main cobblestone street. She looked up at me, her lips parting in surprise, and it took more willpower than I cared to admit to raise my eyes from them.

"To thank you for that remarkable demonstration, how about I treat you to some frozen custard? It is one of my favorite desserts, and perfect for a warm afternoon."

Her lips curled upward, distracting me again. The deep fuchsia color caught my eyes and held them.

"I would love that."

9

Orion

"I believe the king should grant everyone's wishes." Nyra gazed around at the Astorians going about their days with something akin to pity. She ate another spoonful of her lemon-flavored frozen custard, her expression softening as she savored the flavor.

I popped my own laden spoon into my mouth before I could say something I would regret. I let the sharp mint flavor saturate my mouth and melt away as I chose my next words carefully. "There are limits to his magic, too, you know."

She paused, tilting her head to the side in an adorable way that eased my indignation. "There are?"

"How long could you continuously create new illusions before you ran out of magic?" I slowed my steps to match hers.

"I... I am not sure." She frowned. "I have never tried."

"Wish-granting magic is no different from other magics. It does run out. Even the druids, who draw upon the wild magic of nature, can only borrow so much from any single plant or animal without harming it." Some of the tension eased from my shoulders. At least she was receptive, and I could explain it in a way she would understand.

"But I thought that starlight powered the wishes. Was that not why the granting ceremonies are always held at night?"

"From what I have heard, the magic does come from the stars, but not in an unending deluge. It is more of a constant trickle that must be stored up in between wishes, or there will not be enough." It seemed Nyra had been doing her own research.

"So it would take more time to prepare for a wish of a grander scale," she murmured to herself.

Unease stirred in my gut. Would she demand a firm answer from me today? When I said no, would she turn her attentions to some other man who was more willing to champion her cause?

The familiar notes of fiddles and flutes reached my ears, and I latched onto a quick way to change the subject. "Shall we see the musicians?"

The moment Nyra nodded, I took her hand and led her through the crowded streets and to a town square. Although the Wish Festival was still a couple weeks away, people had already begun decorating. Blue and silver ribbons festooned every shopfront and street sign. Folded paper stars hung from the lampposts, their trailing tails fluttering in the breeze like imitations of shooting stars. And starflowers were clustered in every window box, their delicate aromas perfuming the air.

A group of minstrels were performing a lively folk song on the corner, with their crowd of admirers swelling every moment. As I watched, a group of children began to dance to the tune, and they were soon joined by a passionate young couple and a pair of sweet grandparents.

Feeling inspired, I set my empty coldcream cup aside and bowed to Nyra, holding out my hand in invitation. "May I have this dance?"

Her eyes widened in surprise, and she glanced between me and the growing group of dancers nervously. "I am afraid I only know tribal dances."

"Allow me to teach you the dance of my people," I offered. When she hesitated, I smiled encouragingly and added, "It is quite simple. You will pick it up in no time."

Slowly, Nyra bit her lip and nodded, placing her calloused hand delicately in mine. "In that case, I would be delighted to dance with you, Orion."

I drew her close, placing my other hand around her tiny waist. Her lips parted in surprise, and I leaned closer to whisper in her ear, "Just trust me, and follow my lead."

Before she could protest, I swept her into the center of the growing group of dancers. At first she lagged a step behind me, but once she grasped the simple back-and-forth shuffle, she laughed in surprise.

I grinned at the look of delight on her face, and, wanting to hear her sultry laugh again, twirled her around spontaneously. I was rewarded with another laugh, and I made it my mission to keep her smiling as one song bled into the next.

The crowd of dancers around us, the lively tune, and even the clear azure sky all faded into the background as I looked at her. Her dark eyes glittered like endless night beneath her thick eyelashes, and her hair floated wild and untamed around her face, like a dark lion's mane. But it was her alluringly red lips that my eyes kept gravitating towards, like a star circling the sky.

Those mesmerizing eyes dipped to my lips. When she inched closer, tilting her chin ever so slightly upwards, that was all the invitation I needed. Heedless of the dance that continued around us, I pulled her close, spearing a hand through her thick, luscious hair, and pressed my hand into the small of her back until she was flush against me.

I closed my eyes as I kissed her, reveling in the sensation of her velvety soft lips on mine. She tasted like lemon from the frozen custard, with a hint of nutmeg and cardamom. She melted into my touch, and my heart trilled in response.

Was this what love felt like? When I pulled back, my breath caught at the sight of her flushed cheeks and full lips. Stars, she was exquisite. Her half-lidded eyes rooted me to the spot. I went back for more, a drowning man in need of her air.

She wrapped an arm around my neck, and splayed her fingers through my hair. I nearly moaned at the heady sensation. She pressed her lips to mine, her sweetness drowning my senses. And when she pulled back, I tried to follow.

She gave me a husky laugh that made me want to find us a quiet corner somewhere, just for the two of us. Her full lips had my full attention.

"You are not what I expected from an Astorian," she purred, running a hand along my cheek possessively.

"And you are not what I expected from a tribeswoman," I rumbled back, delighting in the look of surprise on her sculpted features when I pushed back, my own hand cupping her velvety-soft cheek.

"So what have you decided, Orion? Will you help me save my people, and my homeland?" Her dark, half-lidded eyes held me captive, just as surely as her lips had mere moments before. Her intoxicating scent urged me to give her the answer I knew she wanted, just so I could stay by her side, basking in her glory.

"Nyra, I will help—"

Another dancer brushed against my shoulder, breaking the spell, and the music and motion around me came crashing back in full force, like a wave breaking on the shore. What had I just been about to promise her? When I glanced up, my gaze snagged on that of a tribesman watching me from the edge of the square. He was a huge, muscular man, and the look he was giving me was anything but friendly.

When I frowned, Nyra followed my gaze, and I heard her breath catch. "Tariq?" she mumbled. I stood a little taller. Did she know that tribesman? What was their relationship?

"Orion!" I startled at the sudden sound of Astrid's voice. Not because I was surprised to see her here, but because of the barely-contained panic in her tone. The last time I had heard such raw emotion from her, we had both nearly lost our lives.

It felt like a bucket of ice-water had been up-ended over my head, dousing the heat Nyra had elicited. Fear shot through my heart like a speeding comet. Had something terrible happened to my family, or one of my guild members? Were they hurt or in danger? I ran to meet Astrid, who wore her bow strapped to her back, dodging through dancing couples to get to her. After a delay, Nyra ran after me, but I had no time to fret over any offense I may have caused at my abruptness.

"Astrid, what is it?" Her hazel eyes flicked over my shoulder at Nyra before returning to me.

"Nova and Castor went to the meeting early!" she exclaimed, waving a piece of paper in my face. "They left a note, explaining that they were going on ahead. They wanted to get that recipe for us, as thanks for you saving Castor's life and for their new apprenticeships!"

My shoulders sagged with relief. "Is that all?" I had feared someone was on the brink of death.

"You do not understand!" Astrid cried, an edge of desperation entering her voice. "Noctus left his report on my desk about that tribesman—and he is not who he says he is! It is *him*, Orion—Khalifon came back! He did not die in the fire!"

"That friend is still alive?!" I snarled, every muscle in my body going taut. Nyra looked at me in alarm.

"Yes! And my apprentices went to see him, *alone!*" Tears of fear glimmered in her eyes. "What if he tries to take them, too?!"

I put a hand on her shoulder, my other resting on the hilt of my sword. "I am not going to let that happen. And this time, we are not going to let him get away."

Astrid stilled at the promise in my eyes. She took a deep breath and bobbed her trembling chin. "I already tried to reach Noctus and Sirius, even Celeste—but no one is answering. You are the first one I could find."

"We cannot wait for them. Did the note say where they were meeting that bastard?" I asked in as calm a tone as I could manage.

"No, but I remember Nova mentioning she found him around the edge of the merchant district, near the starship docks." Astrid's hazel eyes were wide with fear for the two teenagers.

I cursed under my breath. "That is a lot of ground to cover. We had better start running." To Nyra, I said, "I have to go. I—"

"Allow me to come. I can help!" Nyra's chin had that stubborn set to it that I was beginning to recognize.

"We do not have time to argue. Start running!" I almost wanted to ask Astrid to leave this to me, to spare her from having old wounds reopened. But at the same time, I knew she was far too courageous a person to cower from her past when her new apprentices were in danger.

So I grabbed her shaking hand and began to run. Nyra followed behind as we darted out of the square and plunged deeper into the merchant district. But the streets were clogged with people, with no easy way through. I glanced at Astrid and raised an eyebrow. She nodded in confirmation.

"The high way it is."

I squeezed into an alleyway and let Astrid go up the rickety ladder first. Nyra followed her up with little hesitation, and I climbed right after them onto the wood-shingle roof.

"You are not serious," Nyra protested weakly as she looked down over the edge.

"Serious as the stars. If you cannot keep up, you should stay here," I warned her.

She lifted her chin. "I can keep up."

"Good." And with that, Astrid and I ran for the edge of the roof, and vaulted onto the next one.

Nyra stumbled on her landing, and I gritted my teeth in frustration as I pulled her away from the edge. She gave me a nod of thanks, and we continued along our secret pathways, the ones we had used as children, that Noctus had pioneered.

With no people in our way, we made swift progress through the merchant district. Soon, we could see the wish-made lake where the starships rested, their gargantuan masts like a forest of winter-bare trees. Sailors scurried up and down their gangplanks, loading and unloading their precious cargo into the surrounding warehouses.

I slowed my pace as I scanned the streets and the docks for a telltale flash of curly red hair. How were we supposed to find them? They could be anywhere!

"Do you see them?" I asked tersely.

Astrid shaded her eyes with her hand as she searched. "Not yet. But I doubt that man would conduct his business in broad daylight, where all those sailors could see him." Then she paled, dropping her arm as she looked at me. "Do you think...?"

"That he would set up shop in the exact same place?" I cocked my head to the side. "We might as well check."

Astrid swallowed, but nodded. I gave her a tight smile before turning to hop the last few roofs to our destination—a place I had hoped never to visit again. A place I had no doubt still featured in Astrid's nightmares, as they did in mine.

We crept along the roof of the accursed Warehouse 13, which as far as I could tell, had lain empty and abandoned since the fire. I sat down on the edge of the roof near one of its corners, where a semi-rotten length of rope still hung from our previous escape. I slid down it carefully, and held it steady as Astrid and Nyra did as well.

I held my breath as we rounded the corner and stood in the doorless entrance, staring into the belly of the beast. Scorch marks scarred the metal walls and support beams, the cavernous space devoid of the crates of merchandise that filled its neighbors. But the rusted iron cages in the back were the same as I remembered—they even held prisoners again.

Astrid stiffened beside me, and my old helpless fury rose to the surface as I took in the scene before me. Castor lay on the ground, a dark bruise blooming on his face as a mountain of a man I had hoped to never see again held a wailing Nova by the roots of her hair.

He looked up at our entrance, his mis-matched eyes alighting first on Astrid, and then on me. A chilling grin cracked across his face, and the group of men behind him stirred at the look on their leader's face.

"Look what we have here, boys," he sneered. "It's the ones that got away."

10

Orion

I drew my sword, a guttural snarl tearing from deep in my chest. The phantom crack of a whip rang in my ears, the scent of iron and Astrid's screams of pain accompanying it. I stepped in front of her and Nyra protectively, instinctively. Her wide, unseeing eyes told me Astrid was witnessing her nightmares made flesh once more.

I tightened my grip on my sword to force the tremor from my hands. I must show no fear before this monster and his five henchmen. I had to be strong for the both of us.

"Remember Astrid," I quietly said, recalling the phrase I had used to calm her fears the last time we faced this man. "Though darkness falls..."

"Still the stars find their way," she answered, her trembling easing a fraction. We had survived him before, and we would do it again.

"And here I had hoped the fire had done you in." I hardly even recognized my own voice. But no one here expected me to behave like a prince.

"It was close, but I got a nice scar to impress the ladies." His lips twisted in a sneer as he bared his arm towards me. Angry red scars covered much of his limb, shiny and puckered from the heat of the blaze I had once set in this very warehouse.

"You should never have come back, Khalifon." I adjusted my grip on the hilt of my sword, and his eyes tracked the motion.

But he laughed at me, the movement causing Nova to whimper at the tugs on her tender scalp. "And what're you gonna do about it? There's nothing left to burn here!"

"I am a boy no longer." I let my cold fury leak into my tone as I took a step forward, allowing the point of my sword to spark an ember against the rough stone floor. "And I will not allow you to sell another Astrorian child to the mines."

This was what I had been training for, every day, since the last time I had had the misfortune of gazing upon this particular tribesman. Now, I could deliver to him the punishment my younger self had been too small and too weak to dole out.

Khalifon looked down at Castor and then Nova in surprise, A slow, cruel grin spread across his brutish face. "You know this wee boy and his redhead, do you?"

He unsheathed a dagger and brought it to Nova's throat in one easy, practiced motion. "Take one more step, and her hair won't be the only part of her that's red."

I halted, gritting my teeth. As if awoken from a trance, Astrid nocked and drew her bow, the arrowhead pointed at Khalifon's face.

"Get behind us, Castor," she ordered the boy, who quickly scrambled to his feet. Though her voice trembled, her bow remained steady.

"Come to *me* boy, if you want your girlie to keep on breathing." Castor froze, and after a terrified glance at us, moved to stand beside the slaver. I gritted my teeth.

"I am sorry," Nova whispered as tears leaked down her cheeks. Khalifon pressed the dagger against the skin of her throat, silencing her. For an instant, I was a boy again, seeing Astrid held in Nova's place, her hazel eyes wide with hope and fear. Was this what the historians had meant about history repeating itself?

My eyes slid to the handful of children and teenagers watching us from their cages in the back. This time, I had more than just two lives depending on me.

"I thought you were dead. Why would you show yourself now?" I needed to keep him talking.

"Like I could resist such a perfect opportunity as this?" The tribesman laughed, though I noticed his gaze kept straying to Nyra, who was watching this whole exchange silently. "Desperate children, seeking a cure that doesn't exist, but willing to give anything for it?"Despair licked at my mind, but I shoved it aside. Of course a man like Khalifon would not have held the key to curing the plague. I had gotten my hopes up for nothing—for worse than nothing.

"And I see you have a new crew—do they know what happened to your last one?" I called loudly, and was rewarded when they began to scowl and mutter amongst themselves. "If you look carefully, you might still see some of their silhouettes on these very walls!"

When Khalifon looked away and barked at them to be quiet, I narrowed my eyes at Nova and Castor. Castor shook his head imperceptibly, but Nova cut a glare at him, her fierce determination shining through her tears.

I put my free hand behind my back before Khalifon returned his attention to me. I held out three fingers. Folded one back. Then another.

"Nice try," Khalifon sneered. "But if you want to live to see tomorrow, you'll march into your cages." He was openly leering at Nyra now. My rage boiled over, and I cut my gaze to Castor at the same moment that I clenched my hand into a fist.

Astrid's first arrow whizzed past Khalifon's cheek, leaving a fine red line behind before it pinned one of his men against the far wall, like an insect to a display board. The slaver staggered back in surprise, loosening his grip on Nova.

She bit down on his hand as Castor hooked him behind the knees and toppled him like timber. His dagger clattered to the stone floor, and he released Nova's hair so he could catch himself. Wasting no time, Castor gripped Nova beneath the arms and began hauling her towards us, heedless of the hail of arrows Astrid sent streaming past them and into the group of henchmen.

I raced forward, allowing my sword to screech along the stone as I slowly raised the point. Time seemed to slow as the first henchman reached me, an arrow protruding from his shoulder. He brought his sword down towards my head in a vicious strike, which I deflected to the side.

My heart hammered against my ribs as I thrust my blade at his unprotected left side. He brought his guard up just in time, but I used the recoil to bring my own blade around in a quick butterfly arc across his chest. Blood sprayed and he went down, but before I could catch a breath two more were upon me.

I dodged a strike from the left and struck out at the right. Steel rang against steel as he blocked with his short sword, sparks flying at the contact. The faint whistling from behind me was the only warning I got before a longsword cleaved the air where I had just been standing.

The opponent I had just been facing cursed loudly at his comrade, scolding him for nearly catching him up in that last attack. They were clearly unused to working together, which gave me an idea.

Another arrow whistled past my head, followed by a yell of pain. I chanced a quick glance: two men had been felled by Astrid's arrows, and she was now using a continuous stream of them to keep Khalifon at a distance. She was buying me time, but she only had so many arrows in her quiver.

I danced to one side and then immediately jumped into the air as the longsword swept low to the ground, right where my knees had just been. I landed and rolled to the side, coming dangerously close to the tribesman wielding the short sword. I feinted to one side but switched my blade's direction at the final moment, skirting it around his sword so that mine bit into his shoulder.

His yell of pain spurred the other one into motion, and he heaved his longsword up over his head before bringing it down in a devastating, crushing blow. I threw myself out of the way, but the short sword wielder, still reeling from my attack, saw the danger too late.

I spun around and lunged for the longswordsman, who was still staring in shock and horror at what he had done. His weapon was stuck fast, and before he could free it, I slashed my sword across his exposed neck.

"Orion!" Nyra yelled.

"Look out!" Astrid shrieked, and without looking I leaped towards one of the few empty cages, rolling on impact.

"Damn it," muttered Khalifon when his saber clanged against the iron bars, chipping the blade.

I rolled to my feet and brought my guard up just in time to block his next swing. My arm went numb from the jarring impact, and I let out a few silent curses, even as I kept my face carefully neutral. He was nearly as skilled as Sir Rigel, but had far more muscle.

We circled each other, each of us probing for weaknesses. The tribesman's smug look had changed into one of grudging seriousness. But the man had several inches and at least a hundred pounds on me, so I knew I could only block a few more of his strikes, at best. As sweat began to sting my eyes, I knew I had to finish this quickly.

The girls came into view as we continued to circle, and I saw Nyra hugging Nova and Castor close. Astrid's quiver was empty, with just one final arrow nocked and ready.

"You dare look away?" roared Khalifon as he lunged forward, rapidly closing the distance with his saber raised high.

I raised my sword as if to block, but sidestepped at the last possible second. He stumbled, and I used that opening to score my blade across his broad, muscled back. He grunted, but spun to face me, as if he had hardly felt the blow. It had been much too shallow.

"Who...just who are you?" he ground out as we resumed circling. He was watching me warily, his mis-matched eyes narrowed with suspicion. "You fight like a trained knight."

"You should have asked me that question long ago," I growled as I edged around so that Astrid and the others were directly behind me. "Suffice it to say that I am not someone you should have crossed. I would have come for you sooner had I known you survived the fire."

"It was my mistake trying to sell you along with that girl—I should have just killed you both!" Khalifon's face turned a ruddy shade of purple as he lunged forward.

I closed my fist once more and leaned to the left as an arrow whistled through the air where my head had just been. The tribesman's eyes widened in shock, and though he tried to dodge, the blue-fletched arrow sank deep into his chest, a mere inch above his heart. I heard Astrid let out a few choice words at the near miss, but I grinned. That was all the help I needed.

As the slaver reeled back, I rushed forward, bringing my blade to bear on him. My sword was heavy with the weight of my retribution as I rained down a flurry of blows. He grew slower as blood seeped from his wound, and he began to pant heavily from the effort of defending.

He snuck in a few counterattacks, but I ignored the sting in my arm and then my leg as his blade nipped at me. I kept up the pressure, pushing him steadily backwards, towards the iron cages that lined the walls. The smell of smoke and charcoal still clung to them, a fierce reminder of why I had to urge my aching arms to strike *faster*.

I gave him no room to flee, no time to think, no openings to attack. I pushed him back, until there was nowhere left to go. His wounded back hit the bars, and half a dozen small hands clamped tight around his legs and his arms, immobilizing him.

With one final plunge of my blade, I finished what had started so many years ago, when it had been mine and Astrid's faces peering out from behind those bars. The little hands let go, and the slaver slumped to the ground, his blood streaking the iron. My chest heaved, and I could hardly get the air down fast enough.

Cheers and cries of relief went up from the children and teenagers in the cages, their tears cutting through the grime on their faces. I stared blankly at Khalifon's still form, hardly believing that it was finally over.

Two little meteors tackled me in a hug, and I slowly looked down and draped my free hand around Nova's thin shoulders as they shook with silent sobs. Castor wrapped his arms around the both of us, his golden head bowed. Astrid approached next, the shaken look on her face no doubt matching mine. I held out my arm in silent invitation, and I quietly folded her into the hug. She trembled violently as she hid her face against my chest, and I closed my eyes as I tucked her head beneath my chin.

I had never wanted her to have to come here again, to face the harsh reality that had almost been hers. It was the rescue that had started them all, that motivated me to create Hyperion in the first place. Despite the fact that it had also nearly ended my time as Orion before it had truly begun.

I was going to have this entire building razed to the ground, no matter what price the owners demanded from me.

Nyra came and rested a hand on my shoulder, and I was grateful that she waited to ask the questions I knew must be burning on her tongue. I doubted I had any words left in me.

I let out a long, relieved sigh as the adrenaline began to fade. At least everyone was safe. I opened my eyes, and gave a reassuring smile to the dirty little faces looking up at me. Hopefully, Evelyn's Home had enough bedrooms for all of them. And if they did not, I would simply build more.

The thundering of many pairs of boots on cobblestones shattered our quiet reprieve, and my stomach hit my toes when I heard Sir Rigel yell, "By order of the king, you are to drop your weapons and surrender to the Knights of the Evening Star!"

11

Astrid

Orion's arms went rigid around me, and I heard his heart begin to pound anew beneath my cheek. I lifted my tear-blurred eyes to his face, and saw a muscle feathering in his jaw as he stared resolutely ahead. I frowned, wondering why he seemed so alarmed by the royal knights behind us. I had watched him sweet-talk his way past guards and soldiers plenty of times before.

"Orion?" I whispered.

His eyes darted left and right, as if he was looking for a quick escape. Then his gaze alighted on Nyra, and he murmured, "Can you use your magic to glamour us?"

"I can try. But why would you ask? You have done no wrong in stopping these men." She tilted her head to the side in question.

"Then try. Please. I can explain later," Orion hissed. I noticed that he had subtly moved his sword so that its distinctive hilt was hidden behind me, out of view of the knights standing in the entrance.

"I repeat, you are to drop your weapons and surrender to the Knights of the Evening Star!" the lead knight declared as he began to slowly advance into the burned-out warehouse. His group of a half-dozen knights fanned out behind him, and I could see them eyeing the downed and unconscious thugs nervously.

"Orion, why are you hiding your face from them?" I whispered, as Nova and Castor lifted their red-rimmed eyes to watch and Nyra closed hers, and the air around her began to shiver.

"I, uh...I am acquainted with these particular knights." He watched them advance from the corner of his eye. "I do not suppose any of you have the strength to make a run for it?"

Nova gripped Orion's clothes tighter, as if she had no intention of ever letting go. I could hardly blame her. Even now, there was still a tremor in my hands, and I was reluctant to leave the comfort of Orion's arms.

"You boys missed all the fun," Orion called out in a voice far lower than his usual timbre. "We could have used your help about ten minutes ago."

The knights paused, and one in the lead replied, "A passerby notified our patrol of a swordfight."

"Patrol? You guard the castle, not the port. What were you really doing in the area?" Orion's tone was guarded, but I could tell he was stalling for time.

But how did he know these knights if they were from the castle? Had he had a less than ideal encounter with them in Ace's tavern?

"We were already on our way to investigate reports of suspicious activity in the area, as part of an ongoing investigation into the suspicious disappearances of some children," Sir Rigel replied slowly as he crept closer.Nyra frowned in concentration, and the air around us shimmered as if the sun were beating down on us. But when it reached Orion, it fizzled out. Her dark eyes flew open and flicked to the sword still in Orion's hand.

"Is that made of starsteel?" she hissed in alarm. "My mirage will not take hold so long as you are touching it!"

"Damn it all—I forgot. And I have more starsteel than the sword on me, that I cannot remove," he muttered, almost to himself. His shoulders sagged, before he straightened them and set his jaw. He gently extricated himself from me and the two teenagers.

"Please, keep what you are about to see and hear to yourselves." He looked each of us in the eye, waiting until we nodded. The worry in his eyes and the resignation in his tone frightened me, but I gave my assent anyway.

I trusted him.

The knight stepped directly behind Orion, the others fanning out in a semicircle around us. He leveled the point of his sword at Orion's back, and said, "This is your last chance to set down your weapon."

Orion drew himself up to his full height and turned his head slightly over his shoulder, and said in a foreign voice brimming with authority, "You dare point your sword at *me,* Rigel?"

"Your Highness...?" The knight's eyes widened in surprise, and the others began quietly murmuring to themselves. The point of his sword dipped low.

The blood froze in my veins. *What* did he just call Orion?

Orion turned to face the knight fully, planting the tip of his bloodied sword in the ground before him and resting his hands on its hilt. He lifted his chin and looked down his nose at the knight.

"Prince Sterling! What are you..." He looked down at his hand, as if belatedly realizing he was currently committing treason, and immediately sheathed his blade, barking orders at the rest of the knights to do the same. He knelt on one knee before Orion, the others following suit in a wave of motion. "I apologize for not recognizing you, Your Highness. Please forgive my grave transgression."

Nyra's lips parted in surprise, and Nova and Castor were staring slack-jawed at Orion—no, at *Prince Sterling*. His gaze flicked to mine and away again, as if afraid of what he would see in my expression. But all I could do was stare in shock at this person I had known for years, without ever really knowing at all.

"I am disappointed not only with the Order of the Evening Star, but also with myself for allowing these filthy slavers to operate so long, right under our noses." The knights lowered their eyes as Orion swept his gaze over them, though I noticed Sir Rigel's eyes kept darting between me, Nyra and the caged captives behind us.

"You speak as if these tribesmen have operated for years, Highness," Rigel said carefully.

"They have." Prince Sterling's gaze fell on Khalifon's prone form once more.

"Might I be so bold as to enquire how you came to know this, Highness?" This knight must have been particularly close to Orion, based on the way he spoke to him, when the others did not dare to lift their heads.

"Because this is the man who nearly succeeded in selling myself and Astrid to the salt mines in Harland several years ago. Had I known the bastard survived the fire I set during our escape, I would have had him clapped in irons long ago." The prince's voice was cold, colder than I had ever heard it. I saw a grudging respect in Nyra's eyes as she looked at him anew. "This time, he crawled out of the woodwork to lure the desperate in with a false cure for the plague."

Sir Rigel curled his lip in disgust. "Then I am sorry I was not here to assist you in bringing them down."

The prince smiled grimly. "I am grateful for your training. He was nearly as strong as you, Rigel."

The knight's eyes narrowed on the tears in Orion's clothes, and he half-rose. "Highness, you are wounded. Please allow me to—"

"Flesh wounds. They are nothing." He waved off the knight's concerns, and I had to hold myself back from trying to tend to his injuries, as I always had before.

Rigel bowed his head respectfully.

"I now call upon you all, to both break and uphold your oaths," Prince Sterling continued, his voice echoing in the cavernous space.

Sir Rigel raised his head. "Break, Your Highness?"

"I will ask that you fulfill your duty by arresting the slavers still breathing, but that you not mention my hand in this when making your reports to my father."

His father—the King of Astoria.

"Why?" There was a gravitas to Sir Rigel's voice that gave Orion pause.

"Because my father is so afraid of losing me that he would never allow me to set foot in town again," he said softly, but with the force of conviction that I so admired. "But there are things I cannot do while locked away behind the safety of the castle's walls."

Silence met his confession, the air charged with a heady excitement, like the feeling that preceded a lightning strike in a thunderstorm. He had laid his fate at his soldiers' feet, giving them the gift of choice.

"What would you have us say?" Sir Rigel broke the tense silence, and I sensed a wave of relief sweep through the gathered knights. Orion's eyes glimmered with warmth, as if he himself had feared his trust to be misplaced.

"Simply that when you investigated some suspicious individuals, you found the children they had kidnapped." Orion let out a sigh of relief as he gestured at the cages behind him. "And apprehended them in accordance with the law of the land."

The knight drew his sword and held it aloft in front of him, steel whispering on steel as the others did the same. "I, Sir Rigel Gallahad, pledge on my honor as Knight Commander of the Order of the Evening Star, that it will be as you have asked."

Once every knight had made the same pledge, the prince asked the children to keep his secret as well, to which they all eagerly agreed. He gave them a tight smile and turned back to Sir Rigel, who sheathed his sword and finally rose from the ground.

But as my guild master gave instructions on what to do with the children, I stared numbly at his broad back, and covered my mouth with a shaking hand.

Orion was the Crown Prince of Astoria.

The boy I had grown up with, the one who had raced me through the markets and told me stories of the stars... He was royalty. The boy who had grown into a kind and confident leader and guildmaster, who had worked side-by-side with me, treating children with runny noses and orphans with broken bones, was a liar.

He had been lying to my face for as long as I had known him.

No wonder he had never seemed to run out of funds—he had access to the kingdom's treasuries. And here I had assumed he was some sort of successful merchant's son, moonlighting as a guildmaster to help people in secret because his father would have insisted on charging for such services.

Something clicked in my mind. Orion's so-called miracles—he must have been granting wishes! It made perfect sense. Only the king—or, I supposed, the prince—had the power to grant other's wishes.

How had I never seen it before?

His refusal to talk about his personal life, his insistence on code names related to the stars, his intricate knowledge of the kingdom's laws and how they were enforced... It all made perfect sense. Perfect, ridiculous sense.

I bit my salty lip. What a fool I was, to have fallen in love with the prince who had saved me.

Why had he never told me? Did he think so little of me? That I was incapable of keeping his secrets, after everything he had done for me? When I owed the man my life?

A single tear streaked down my face.

If he had not told me by now...I doubted he had ever planned to do so. And what was he going to do about his guild, our family, when he became king? One day, would he have simply stopped coming, leaving us to fear the worst and continue on in his stead?

Had I ever truly known him, or had everything been a carefully-fabricated lie?

My throat constricted, and a sudden realization struck me like lightning. Guilt clenched my heart in starsteel talons, replacing the sense of betrayal I felt. If Orion was the prince, then...

Did he know that the girl he had so selflessly saved was the very reason he had lost his mother?

12

Orion

"I would like all of the rosemary, yarrow, and cometbloom that you have available." I rested my hands on the apothecary's counter as I scanned the dozens of small drawers that lined the wall, each impeccably labeled with its contents and a date.

Now that my hopes of a cure from the desert had been brutally dashed, we were back to square one. And that meant pinning all of my hopes on Astrid creating her own cure—even if she had refused to so much as look at me since she had learned of my true identity.

"The rosemary and cometbloom will not be a problem, but I am afraid we have only two bundles of yarrow left," replied the clerk

I blinked. "Only two?"

"Since it is you, Orion...I will tell you why." The clerk lowered her voice to a whisper. "Due to this mysterious plague, everyone is searching for a cure. And since none of the herbalists have discovered one yet, the desperate are trying to make their own. We can hardly keep half our herbs in stock."

I leaned in closer as well. "Can you estimate how many cases you have heard of?"

"At least three dozen in the last week—and that does not include all those purchasing herbs at the other apothecaries."

"It must be spreading faster," I murmured grimly.

She nodded. "Our only hope now is for someone," she paused, glancing pointedly at me, "to come up with a cure."

"I can make no promises, but rest assured, I am working on it." The words were barely a whisper, for the clerk's ears only. I did not want to raise false hope in the few other customers currently browsing.

But the clerk beamed at me all the same as she retrieved the requested herbs and handed them over. "On the house."

I set a gold coin, far more than the herbs were worth, on the counter and slid it towards the clerk. "I appreciate the gesture. Please, use this to cultivate or acquire as many herbs as you possibly can."

"Thank you. It will not go to waste." Her eyes sparkled with emotion, and her chin quivered for a moment.

I left with a wave. I hoped the coin would help to tide the apothecary over, for a little while at least. I had the sneaking suspicion that unless Astrid discovered a cure within the next few days, things were going to get far worse before they got better.

As both a prince and a guildmaster, I needed to do more for my people. If that meant draining the amulet every night, then so be it. Even if it grated on my nerves every time.

I paused to glance into the windows of a bakery, using the angle of the glass to take a peek at the man who had followed me out of the apothecary. He, too, paused in front of a window, stroking his beard and doing a poor job of feigning disinterest. He was older, in his mid-forties, with salt-and-pepper hair. Laugh lines marked the corners of his green eyes and a scar divided one of his eyebrows. His clothes were worn but well-cared for, and he seemed incredibly fit for his age, which made me wonder if he was a soldier.

I continued walking, and heard his measured steps tap out an answering rhythm on the cobblestones. Most would never dream of tailing Orion the guildmaster through the streets. Did that make him a foreigner? Or had he somehow overheard my conversation with the apothecary clerk?

If that was the case, then I should avoid confronting him in the streets. Casually, I turned down a narrow alley. I grimaced as I tucked the herbs into my satchel so I could draw my starsteel blade. I had been spending far too much time in dark alleys lately.

When the man rushed around the corner, I was ready and waiting for him. His eyes flew wide in surprise, and he quickly raised his hands in the air.

"For what reason are you following me?" I growled. I needed to make this quick, so I could deliver these herbs to Astrid.

"To thank you," the man blurted out. He scratched at his head almost sheepishly. "I just, ah—you seemed quite busy, so I was simply trying to find an appropriate moment to approach you."

I kept my sword raised.

"And why would you be thanking me? As far as I can recall, this is our first meeting." I was certain I would have remembered this man if I had granted his wish.

"You saved my Brian, the boy with the crushed leg. I never thought he would walk again." Emotion choked the big man's voice, and he cleared his throat with some embarrassment.

I sheathed my sword, but kept my hand on the hilt. "Are you the boy's father?" I vaguely recalled healing the boy—that had been a few nights before the confrontation with Khalifon, so I had not given the incident a second thought.

"Yes. My name is Leonidas. I was away at the starship ports in Delphini on business when it happened, and only returned this morning. He told me what you did for him." The man cleared his throat again. "And I...wanted to express my gratitude to you myself. I do not know what you did, but it worked."

"I was happy to help." I finally relaxed my stance, relieved the boy had kept his promise—and my secret.

"How can I repay you?" the man pressed. I held up a hand.

"No repayment is necessary. That is not the reason I help people." I felt a flicker of magic, so I grabbed my watch and snapped it open. Sure enough, there was a starnote from Noctus, letting me know that he had found more plague victims for me to help. I grimaced and fired off a quick reply that I was on my way back, before returning the watch to my pocket. "If you will excuse me, I am expected elsewhere."

I began to walk past Leonidas, but he put a hand on my shoulder. "Let me join you."

"Pardon?"

"Let me join Hyperion." His gaze was steady, his tone serious.

"I told you, no repayment is necessary." But I eyed the grizzled man with renewed interest. Plenty of people had asked to join my guild in a fit of gratitude, but I allowed very few people to actually join the guild. They had their own lives to live, after all. Most I simply asked to provide Hyperion with information or services.

"I want to help people the way you helped Brian." His grip tightened.

"Why?"

"I grew up in Harland. I served my time in the salt mines, and in the army, as all subjects are called to do. Most people, myself included, were miserable, barely able to scrape together enough coin to feed ourselves and our families." His gaze darkened, and I sensed some unspoken sorrow in him.

"I did not realize it was so bad over there." We conducted little trade with them, and like us, they were too busy dealing with attacks from witches and tribesmen to bother with nonaggressors.

He nodded gravely. "But Astoria is a whole different realm. Free trade, no conscription, relative safety...and even the opportunity to have a wish granted by the king! However, as of late, the influx of tribesmen and women, and the spreading of this wretched plague have been causing the kind of unrest common in Harland. But unlike in *that* kingdom, there are people in this one who are trying to protect both Astoria and her people. Like you."

"You want to keep Astoria from becoming like Harland," I stated softly.

"Though I have only lived here for a handful of years, even I can clearly see the danger knocking at the door. This place, these people, must be protected. It is by no means perfect, but I have faith Prince Sterling will continue his father's legacy and usher in an even greater era of prosperity. But if things continue going as they are, I fear the Kingdom of the Stars will fall." Leonidas' sincerity surprised me. How was it that a foreigner had more faith in me, the prince, than most of my own people?

Perhaps it was exactly because he had seen the results of Harland's governance that he so appreciated ours. I could not help the smile that curved my lips, despite his dire prediction, which echoed my own fears.

Fears the king continually dismissed.

"Why do you wish to join my guild, instead of work for the royals you hold in such high regard?" It seemed an odd choice to me.

"I suppose you could say the reason is because I have seen firsthand the tangible good you do. I was aware of you long before you helped Brian, and I have learned of the results of your efforts, of just how many lives have been saved or bettered by your hand. And yet, you are always on the lookout for more people to help—which is why I have seen you frequenting so many taverns, pretending to sip your ale." He gave me a knowing look.

I laughed aloud, my hand finally leaving my sword. The man really had been paying attention, if he was wise to my ways. He was a kindred spirit, if he was so eager to enact the kind of immediate, meaningful change that could only be created on an individual level.

"Luckily for you, I could use an advisor. Welcome to the guild, Leo." I held out my hand, and after a moment of stunned silence, he took it.

"I am happy to be of service, Orion." His hands were rough and calloused, testifying to his veteran status.

I had a feeling I stood to learn a lot from him, and perhaps him from me.

"Walk with me, Leo." I led the way out of the alley and back onto the busy streets, and Leo fell in beside me. "Just out of curiosity, how did you come to find me today?"

"Ah, that. I knew you had been frequenting apothecaries as of late; it was simply a matter of visiting each one until I caught a glimpse of you." He rubbed the back of his neck.

"Have you deduced why?" It would be a problem if word had already gotten out about what I had Astrid working on.

"Hyperion sells a good deal of effective remedies and healing tonics to the apothecaries and herbalists in town." Leo glanced around before lowering his voice. "But based on your other activities, and the range of herbs you have been purchasing lately, I would imagine you are attempting to find a solution to one of Astoria's most pressing problems."

I dipped my chin in a shallow nod, wincing internally. It might be wiser to send our lesser-known members on these errands from now on.

"Has much progress been made?" The hope in his voice was exactly why I wanted to keep this project secret.

"Not much, yet. But if anyone can find one, it will be Astrid." Leo did his best to hide his disappointment. I knew how he felt.

When we arrived at the guild, Sirius opened the door, Estelle peeking out from behind his legs. His brown hair was shaggy and tousled, as if he had just awakened from a nap—or had been coerced into a game of make-believe with a certain little one.

"Is he here for a miracle?" Estelle blurted out.

I smiled down at her, giving a subtle nod to Sirius. "No, this is Leo—he is the newest member of Hyperion."

Estelle pouted. "But you promised to play Shooting Stars with me today!"

"Why, that is one of my favorite games! May I join in, little star?" Leo exclaimed as he crouched down in front of her. He glanced up at Sirius, seeking permission first, which Sirius gave. Based on the look in his eye, Leo had already won him over.

She gave him an appraising look, before beaming at him. "You can be the shooting star first!"

"You three get started, and I will join once I give these to Astrid." I strode down the hall, but Astrid and Nova met me halfway.

"I told you to come back with some herbs, not a new member," Astrid took the bundle as she eyed Leo. Her tone was cold, and she refused to meet my eyes.

"Now I am no longer the newest member!" Nova grinned, before bounding forward to join the game. She seemed tired, but in good spirits. I knew she would bounce back from her ordeal quickly, even if the bruise on her face would take longer to heal.

"What can I say—he wanted to help." We both turned to watch him chase Estelle around the room, pretending that he was struggling to catch her. Astrid's expression softened as she watched how good the older man was with Estelle. The sight made me want to spend more time with my own father. My memories of time spent with him, playing games and telling stories, were my most cherished.

"He is who he says." Noctus appeared at my elbow, silent as a wraith.

"You are far too distrusting, Orion," Astrid murmured. I winced at the barbed comment.

"Thank you for checking." I would not risk my guild members' safety. "And the rest?"

"Those stricken with the plague rarely recover naturally. Thirteen new cases, just today. And..." Noctus hesitated, which was unlike him.

"What is it?" I questioned, dreading the answer.

"Several black markets have popped up, with swindlers claiming to sell potions that can cure the plague. The price of a single vial is the buyer's wish."

I swore.

"And the potions are bogus, I presume?" Astrid asked flatly.

"Of course." Noctus seemed even more glum than usual.

"If they had been effective, I could have traded my wish for one, so I could use it to learn to make my own," Astrid murmured.

"You would do that?" I asked in surprise.

"Yes. Others need it more than I." Her half-smile was strained.

"You amaze me every day." But then I sighed. "Black markets for wishes were never meant to happen."

Astrid pinned me with a look. "Unfortunately, the original intentions are far less important than the tangible results they bring about."

I knew she was talking about more than just the black markets. I felt her words strike home, gutting me. But I supposed I preferred passive aggressiveness to the cold shoulder. But how could I possibly bridge the growing divide between us?

13

Orion

"Why not delegate more of your tasks to your guild members?" Leo asked. "That would allow you to focus more on looking at the big picture."

I *had* delegated a good deal, but there were always things I simply could not leave to others, not without revealing too much. Besides, I was leery of letting anyone else so much as glimpse the star sapphire pendant, let alone attempt to wield its magic. That would be a disaster waiting to happen.

We strolled through the market district, blending in with the other shoppers in the late afternoon. I had sent Leo in to purchase additional herbs for Astrid to use, since I was becoming too recognizable—and predictable, as of late.

Word was finally out about how I could cure the plague, which meant I was mobbed every time I was recognized. The most I could do was direct them to one of Hyperion's new receiving rooms, which were often hidden in plain sight at various apothecaries. Leo had been instrumental in setting those up, and they had already been a great help.

I hesitated. Leo's words echoed the ones I had spoken time and again to my own father. Had I been failing to take my own advice?

"You trust them, do you not?" Leo prompted when I failed to answer right away.

Did I? I trusted them with Orion's life, certainly. But what of Prince Sterling's? Could I trust them with the secrets I carried, secrets that could bring my kingdom to its knees? Though that choice had been made for me, at least where a few people were concerned.

Before I could reply, screams and shouts reached my ears. I shared a glance with Leo, and we both took off running in the direction of the commotion. A crowd was forming near the mouth of an alley, but I shoved my way through to see a young boy screaming at a bearded tribesman.

The boy was no more than twelve. Tears poured down his face, and the flimsy knife he held out in front of him trembled. His clothes were worn and patched, but there was no fear in his brown, furious eyes as he faced down the tribesman.

"Give her back, you liar!" the boy screamed, pointing his knife at the man.

I narrowed my eyes, attempting to place the man in my memories. He looked familiar, but where had I seen him before? He sported a thick beard, as most tribesmen did, and wore their traditional dress of loose pants and a fitted vest. He scowled at the boy, curling his lip in distaste, and the memory suddenly clicked.

This was the tribesman who had been glaring at me when I was dancing with Nyra in the town square. The one whose gaze had darkened when I placed my hand around her waist.

"I gave you what you asked for, boy! It is not my fault if you administered the tonic incorrectly," he sniffed derisively.

"No! No, you promised your desert remedy would cure my sister of the plague! But it did nothing, and now she is dead!" The sheer agony in his voice felt like a punch to the gut, and the tribesman belatedly began to notice how the gathered crowd began to whisper and glare at him.

It seemed Khalifon had not been the only con man selling false hope.

"*You* were the one who assumed it would cure her. I made no such promises." He finally had the good sense to look nervous.

"I gave you my wish to save my sister! You took both of them from me, and now I want them back, Tariq!" The boy advanced a step, and Tariq's hand drifted towards the saber at his hip.

"Leo, protect the boy," I ordered as I stepped forward, out of the crowd.

The veteran soldier made for the child as I strode towards Tariq. I heard Leo trying to comfort the boy, to usher him away from the tribesman.

"Touch one hair on that boy's head and I will make you wish you had never set foot in Astoria." My tone was soft, but Tariq scowled at the threat.

"The brat has done nothing to deserve such an item." His dark eyes were filled with malice and envy.

"That is not for you to decide, foreigner," I hissed, then raised my voice. "Return what you took from the boy, or I will report you to the guards for unlawful entry to the country and fraudulent business practices."

The crowd pressed in closer, a group of muscled blacksmiths and journeymen stepping menacingly to the forefront. Tariq's eyes flicked this way and that, looking for an escape route, no doubt. But he was boxed in, surrounded by angry Astorians.

I saw the moment he realized there was only one way out of this situation for him. "Fine," he ground out, as he reached inside of his vest and withdrew the starsteel pendant and held it out to me.

I stretched out my hand, and he dropped the necklace onto my palm. I closed my fist around the cold steel, never taking my eyes off of him. I heard quiet sobbing from behind me, and gritted my teeth. The tribesman could return the boy's wish, but it was too late for his sister.

"I had better not catch you doing this again," I warned, as he turned away.

Tariq paused, and said without turning around, "You will get what is coming to you, Orion. And when that time comes, you will rue this day."

And with that, he shoved his way through the crowd, which parted before him, as if no one wanted to be near his foulness. I did not blame them. His parting words had rattled me more than I cared to admit, but I tried to push them out of my mind as the empty threats of the defeated.

I nodded my thanks to the men who had stepped forward. They returned the gesture before going back to their own work, and I turned to approach Leo and the boy.

"Here," I said as I held out the pendant to him. The starsteel glittered in the late afternoon light, the faint whisper of its magic responding to the pendant concealed beneath my clothes.

The boy stared at the necklace. Leo put a hand on his back, and the boy finally took it. "Thank you," he whispered hoarsely. Tears still leaked from his reddened eyes.

"Where are your parents? We can take you back to them," Leo offered gruffly.

"They died. The plague took them. My sister was all I had left, until the sickness took her too." His face screwed up with pain. "They should have saved their wishes! Then they might still be alive!" His laugh was devoid of humor. "Not that the king would have granted them in time, anyways."

Leo and I exchanged glances. I knelt down in front of the boy, and waited until he looked at me.

"I can bring you to an orphanage that is run by good people. They can take care of you there, just until you come of age—" I started, but the boy shook his head.

"I will not go." He glared in the direction Tariq had gone.

"Lad, killing that swindler will not bring them back," Leo said softly. I had a feeling he was speaking from experience, and I think the boy could tell, too.

His shoulders slumped. "Then what am I supposed to do?"

"Join Hyperion. Help us prevent what happened to you from happening to others," I offered.

His eyes narrowed with hatred. "Where were you when they were all still alive? You could have saved them! I know what they say about you, that you can cure anything!"

I winced. Leo made as if to protest, but I waved him off. I knew the lad was just looking for someone else to blame.

"Unfortunately, I am only one person. If I had more help, perhaps I could have found your family in time," I said sadly. "But I did not, and I am sorry for that." I refused to look away from the accusation in his eyes. He was not wrong—I might have saved this boy's family, if only I had known of their plight.

Leo had been right. It was far past time I expanded the guild and delegated more, so this boy's story would not be repeated.

The anger drained from the boy's face, and his shoulders caved inwards.

"I can offer you room and board, and a good wage. But more than that, I can offer you the opportunity to help us save as many as we can, so no one else has to go through what you just did." I placed a hand on his trembling shoulder.

He nodded in acceptance.

"What should we call you, lad?" Leo asked.

He shook his head. "I care not what you call me."

His name would only remind him of what he had lost, of those who had used to call him by it. I could understand that.

"Cosmo. From now on, your name is Cosmo. He who protects."

"Welcome home, Orion," Celeste greeted me as I walked into the guild, with Leo and Cosmo. She tossed her long blonde hair over one shoulder, and I noticed Noctus' eyes track the motion before darting away again. The poor boy had been enamored with Celeste since the day she joined Hyperion.

"Thank you for all your hard work, Celeste. We have a new guild member, Cosmo, starting today." I smiled warmly at her as she waved to a shy Cosmo, whose cheeks turned pink. It looked like Celeste had acquired another admirer.

I nodded at guild members and clients alike as I moved through the halls, breathing in the musty air. This place had always felt more like a home than the castle, and I treasured every moment I was here.

"Leo will help you settle in," I told Cosmo, who was peering around at the present guild members, though his eyes kept returning to Celeste.

"You can have the room right next to mine. I will get you some fresh blankets." Leo put his hand on the boy's back and guided him down the hall, towards the spare rooms.

Sirius, who had opened the door for us, crossed his arms over his chest, an inscrutable look in his eyes. "He is a lot like me. Except instead of having you offer me my salvation by saving my sister, a conman got to him first."

I sighed. "There are just too many of them, especially now that this plague seems to be spreading even faster. Even with the new request boxes, we are not finding them fast enough."

"If only there were more Orions running around," Sirius said with a sad smile. "Is there anything you can do for him?"

I shook my head. "If the sister has already departed this world, then there is nothing I, nor anyone else, can do to bring her back."

"Then I pray to the stars that Cosmo will find some measure of solace in preventing the same fate from befalling others." Sirius fell silent, his gaze boring into mine. "And I will try to do for him what you have done for me."

A lump rose in my throat as Sirius clapped a hand on my shoulder. I nodded, and after a moment, managed to say, "Thank you."

That conversation echoed in my mind as I left the guild house and walked to the tavern where I was to meet Nyra this evening.

It was a rare thing for Sirius to be so open with me, but I felt reassured that between him and Leo, Cosmo was in good hands.

I arrived first, so I ordered our usuals from Ace, and sat down at a table in the back. Astrid and everyone else had been working so hard lately that it felt strange to try and relax. But I needed to talk to Nyra about what she had learned in the warehouse. Nova and Castor had been quick to take an oath of silence, but both Astrid and Nyra had remained unnervingly silent on the matter. Hopefully, they both simply needed some time to think.

Astrid's reception at the guild earlier had been rather frosty, though Nova and Castor treated me no differently. But could I blame her for that reaction? I had known this would happen—that was part of the reason I had never worked up the courage to tell her the truth before. I rubbed my temple, trying to fend off a growing headache.

It felt like everything was spiraling out of control. Khalifon and every other cure-peddling tribesman I had encountered just this afternoon had only raised more false hope. My secret was finally starting to leak, the plague was spreading, and we still had no cure to rely on, except for the amulet and its limited magic capacity.

"Hello, handsome," purred a familiar voice, and I smiled in relief at Nyra as she pecked my cheek. At least she was not upset with me.

"Good to see you, gorgeous." I slid a drink over to her as she sat down across from me. "Your perfume is lovely, as always."

"I am glad you think so. It is my favorite, after all." She ran a hand through her long hair, and the sweet scent intensified. My head throbbed, but I refrained from wincing.

"Nyra, I…were you aware that some tribesmen have been selling fake plague remedies in exchange for wish pendants?" I blurted out. Normally, I tried to be a bit more subtle, but I needed to know, and I was growing to trust Nyra more and more as we spent time together. In truth, I knew I was stalling.

She stilled.

"They are?" She frowned, and I was honestly relieved to see that she was also upset by such actions, given her desire to have her own wish granted. "Fret not, Orion. I will speak to them about this."

"There have been quite a few similar incidents as of late. Would you have any idea why tribesmen and women are suddenly so keen on acquiring wish pendants?" I watched carefully for her reaction.

"Hmmm. Must be a few bad apples among the refugees, who are hoping to establish lives for themselves here, with the kind of assistance a wish can bring," Nyra said slowly, in between sips of her mead. "I would not worry so much."

Not worry? Cosmo's devastated face flashed through my mind. He was only one of dozens who had fallen prey to such schemes. Every one of them were faced with both the loss of their loved ones and their wish pendants, not to mention the betrayal of their most desperate and sincere hopes.

Before I could argue, Nyra lowered her voice and murmured, "So, should I call you Orion or Sterling?" She batted her eyelashes at me.

"Orion. And, ah, you have not...mentioned this to anyone, right?" I tapped a finger against my tankard.

"Of course not. I always take care of my own," she purred.

"I appreciate that." She considered me hers? Heat rose unbidden in my cheeks. Had I been worried for nothing?

"It must have been Ashra's divine providence that led me to meet you that day."

"Ashra?" I asked.

"The Goddess of the Rain and the Oasis." Nyra beamed. "She led me to the very person who can help me save my people."

I blinked. When had I agreed to do that? My head throbbed, and I pushed my untouched mead away. How could I possibly deny her request now that she knew who I was?

"Have you had a chance to speak to your father about aiding the Tribes?" she went on.

I worked my jaw, and took a calming breath before I replied, "No, not yet. The next Wish Festival and the influx of emergency wish requests have been occupying most of his time."

"The next Wish Festival is soon?" Nyra perked up.

"Next week. I believe he will be open to granting a few additional wishes this quarter—given current circumstances."

Not that that would be even close to the number that was now needed.

"I have heard tales of these festivals. The locals speak of night markets filled with wondrous foods and trinkets, as well as some kind of light display on the final night." I relaxed a fraction at the excitement in her voice, in her doe-like eyes.

"The rumors are true. It will last for a week, with a few wishes being granted each night. The merchants all create food and goods just for the night market. To conclude the festivities, the castle shoots starlight-infused powder into the night sky, and they explode in beautiful patterns. We call them starbursts." I smiled as I recalled my favorite part of the festival. I never tired of the display, no matter how many times I saw it.

"I look forward to it." Then Nyra batted her eyelashes at me, placing her hand over mine. "Though, I imagine I would enjoy it far more if I were not alone..."

"Would you...like to go with me to the festival on the final night?" I asked, taking the hint.

"Absolutely! I am looking forward to our date."

14

Astrid

I gasped when I saw a star appear on Orion's skin through a tear in the back of his tunic. He winced as the star grew brighter, as if it were burning him. My hand flew to my mouth as I slowly, quietly stepped away from the tiny window that Orion had covered with a cloth, and the small gap that had been just wide enough for one eye to peer through.

Quickly, I hurried back to my workshop, shutting the door securely behind me. I sank down into my chair, my gaze rising to the glittering stars that were framed so perfectly by my window.

The wisps of starlight that had surrounded the young boy as Prince Sterling granted his wish had left me in awe. Earlier, I had hardly been able to hold a simple conversation with the stranger I knew so well, so how was I meant to face him *now?*

The prince-turned-guildmaster who spent his nights wiping the runny noses of orphans and saving those in need?

It made no sense and made perfect sense at the same time.

This must be why he almost always came here at night—as far as anyone could tell, granting wishes had to be done at night, when the starlight was strongest. But why was he going around, granting wishes in secret?

Would it not make more sense for him to simply hold more frequent Wish Festivals? And why hide his identity, when his title would have opened so many doors for him, and granted him the immediate respect and obedience of everyone he came across?

Was he worried about his own safety? No, there was no way that was the reason. Orion always carried a starsteel sword at his hip—he was by no means defenseless, as evidenced by how he defeated that monster, Khalifon. If he cared more for his own health than that of others, he would fear going near those stricken with illness. But he was always the first to volunteer to help me tend to the ill.

Then I remembered what he had said to those knights, that day in the warehouse. I had nearly forgotten: everything after his initial revelation that day was rather blurry.

Of course the king would not have allowed his sole son and heir to go about in the city, granting the wishes of the people alone and unguarded. Was he simply concerned for his son's safety? Or was there some other reason?

My mind flashed back to that night at the orphanage, when the guildmaster had winced when Nova hugged him. At the time, I had believed him when he said that the girl had simply agitated a wound he had sustained from training. But now that I thought back, over all of the nights Orion had performed his "miracles" to save someone, there had been many occasions when he seemed to be in pain. Many times when I had noticed how he went out of his way to have nothing near his back.

I stilled as realization dawned on me.

Wish-granting magic and all it entailed had always been kept shrouded in mystery. Little was known about it, outside of the basic, visible results it generated. And most people were content to leave the subject alone, so long as their wishes continued to be granted.

But I was one of only a handful of people who knew that the late queen had breathed her last *while granting a wish*. Guilt and fear shivered down my spine, and I wrapped my arms around myself.

I gazed at the cold stars that littered the heavens, like so many crystals in the night. Their distant beauty always made me feel so small, so alone. And I always wondered if at least one of them resented me. I would not blame her if she did.

Of course granting wishes came with a cost. *All* magic required something of its wielder, and star magic was no exception. But no one who wanted their wish to be granted would dwell on the price *someone else* had to pay to make their dream into reality.

Myself included.

What price had the prince been paying all this time? Was it as simple as physical pain? Or was it something far more than that, something beyond what the eye could see?

A lump rose in my throat.

Orion had stepped forward hundreds of times over the last few years, to pick up where my remedies failed. The stars swam in my vision as it dawned on me that every single time, Orion had had to pay the price for someone else's salvation. And he had done it gladly, willingly, with a smile on his face, every single time.

And not once had he ever complained.

No wonder his goal was to reduce people's reliance on wishes.

Perhaps that was the reason only the king had led each and every Wish Festival. After all, what good parent would ever want to see their child suffer? To live with the guilt of shifting that burden to their child to lessen their own pain?

But for the prince to take on that responsibility then in secret, to shield his father from that painful knowledge and to lessen that burden... My heart ached.

Would I have had the courage to do what Orion did? I laughed to myself, a broken sort of sound. No. I did not even have the courage to tell Orion the truth, let alone face the problems I had been running from my entire life.

A knock sounded at the door, startling me from my spiraling thoughts. My heart jumped—was it Orion at the door? Had he spotted me peeking? Quickly, I swiped at my cheeks and tried to quietly clear the lump in my throat.

"Come in," I called softly, only the slightest quiver in my voice.

I held my breath as the door was eased open, and let out a sigh of both relief and disappointment when I recognized my visitor. Noctus slipped inside and closed the door behind him, his light footfalls undetectable to human ears.

"Noctus, what brings you here? Did you need a remedy?" I crossed my legs, playing with my dull brown hair.

"I know." His dark gaze pierced mine, and it felt like he could peer into my soul. It was one of the quirks that made him so skilled at gathering information.

"You know? Know what?" Had he seen me spying on the guildmaster? Was he going to report me for insubordination, have me banished from the guild?

But I was not ready to face Orion yet! What could I possibly say to him?

"That you have learned of the guildmaster's secret." The quiet man took one menacing step forward, and I flinched. I had never felt afraid of Noctus before, but I did now. At least, until he added, "As well."

I blinked.

"You knew?"

He nodded.

"For how long?" I whispered. My mind spun, re-examining all of his interactions with Orion, but found nothing amiss.

"I pieced it together not long after I joined." His dark eyes noted my every movement, his gaze appraising.

"But...that was years ago! Why have you never said anything?" I stared at the man like I had never seen him before.

I hated that that was becoming a familiar feeling. First Orion, now Noctus... Who was next? Celeste?

"It was never my secret to tell." The simplicity of his answer surprised me. "Besides, he seems so much happier and relaxed when he is here. I would never want to take that away from him."

"Fair enough." I would not want to cause Orion pain, either. Then I thought for a moment. "Then you must also know...what his so-called "miracles" really are."

"I do."

"Does that mean he granted your wish, and that became your reason to join the guild?" That would make sense, if Noctus had joined out of a feeling of indebtedness to Orion.

"No, nor have I asked. He just..." Noctus sighed, seemingly lost for words. "I was in a dark place when he found me. He saved me from myself, and I chose to follow him, to help him reach others like me."

Now it was Noctus who was fidgeting. I had never known the man to volunteer any personal information before. Despite the fact that we were around the same age, he had always given off an air of wanting to be left alone, and I had respected that.

"Everyone here owes him their lives, in one way or another," I said softly. That familiar sense of gratitude welled up in my chest, dispelling some of my confusion and hurt, even if that emotion was now tempered with guilt.

Noctus nodded solemnly, the understanding in his eyes making me want to squirm. I had little doubt Noctus already knew all about our recent encounter with Khalifon, and therefore, all about my own story.

"How did you find out?" I tilted my head to the side.

"Master of information-gathering, remember?" Noctus gave me a lop-sided smile. "He hides it well, but everyone makes mistakes."

"True." I gave him a tentative smile, which he returned.

My smile dimmed as I glanced at the stars once more. "Do you know? Have you been able to learn what price it is he pays every time he grants a wish?"

Noctus let out a breath, his eyes following my gaze to the stars. "Not entirely. I am absolutely certain physical pain is part of it, but the king has been so careful with anything regarding wish-granting magic that even I have not been able to find out much."

"He winced after he cured those at the orphanage of the plague, when Nova hugged him and touched his back. And just now, I saw the shape of a star appear on his skin. It almost looked as if it were...burning him." My eyes cut to Noctus', and I saw my own sympathy etched on his usually stoic features.

"I have noticed that as well. He has gotten much better at hiding it, but it pains him every time. The more wishes, the bigger the wish...the more it seems to hurt him." Noctus nodded to himself.

"What if..." I rushed ahead before I had time to second-guess myself. "What if the reason the king has refused to allow the prince to take over wish-granting is because he does not want his son to pay that price?"

Noctus' eyes widened, then narrowed. "You suspect part of the price to be a sliver of the user's life."

I nodded, my throat closing. Some part of me had hoped Noctus, knowledgeable as he was, would brush off my concerns. But based on the look on his face...

"It could be possible. Look at what the witches' magic does to *them*. It ages them, wrinkling their skin and weakening their bones." He began pacing back and forth, his agitation infectious. I began fiddling with my braid again, the enormity of the situation settling on my shoulders like a boulder.

"Even the wild magic of the druids can turn on them. Asking a vine to snare an enemy will cause it to wither away afterwards, all of its energy spent. And healing a fox's injured paw would be pointless if you had to use up its lifeforce to do so. All magic comes at a cost." I knew that better than most, so how had I never noticed before?

Then Noctus whirled on me. "Does anyone else know?" The panic in his voice unnerved me.

I paused, then nodded. "Some of the castle's knights, including Sir Rigel, plus Nova and Castor. And...Nyra."

Noctus cursed. "The knights are one thing, but the tribeswoman...

I stiffened. "Have you looked into her?"

"Yes."

"And?" I demanded.

"There are plenty of eye-witnesses to her sowing discontent since she first came to Astoria. But there is practically no information on her from before that point," he replied grimly.

"How is that possible?"

"My guess? Either she created a new identity for herself, or someone very powerful has taken great care to withhold her information." His tone told me how unusual that was.

Why had a few more people knowing Orion's true identity worried Noctus to such a degree? Did he doubt their integrity? But why bring that up when we were discussing the magic's price?

I paled. "You suspect that someone else knows, or at least suspects, the price of a wish. And are purposefully spreading this plague." Horror roiled through me.

A few weeks ago, I might have been only somewhat bothered by this revelation. But now that I knew it was *my* guildmaster paying this price, and being targeted by this scheme...

"Without a cure for the plague..." Noctus trailed off, looking at me meaningfully.

"The prince and the king will both be drained dry." I swallowed. "I will be putting everything else on hold. Nova and Castor can handle making the minimum number of potions for the apothecaries, so I will be moving my focus to helping me with creating a cure immediately."

"Thank you. I can get as many water and garment samples from the affected as you need. Whatever it takes." Noctus' tone was solemn and calm, but I noted the way a muscle feathered in his jaw.

I nodded my thanks. If only I had access to my full abilities... Perhaps then I could heal the sickness, or at least grow a new crop of the herbs I needed every week. No, I refused to render the queen's sacrifice meaningless. There was no point in dwelling on what I lacked. Instead, I squared my shoulders.

"Find and bring in as many plague victims as you can. The more we help now, the less it will spread. And hopefully...the less it will cost Orion." I locked gazes with Noctus, seeing my own determination reflected there.

Here was my opportunity to truly repay both Orion and his father for what they had done for me...

And for what I had cost them.

15

Orion

"How is that lady-friend of yours these days, Highness?" Sir Rigel grunted as he parried my blow.

The distraction tactic worked, and I fumbled my sword in surprise. The knight grinned, and I barely brought up my guard in time. Splinters flew from our wooden practice weapons.

"She is well," I replied evenly, trying not to let thoughts of her mesmerizing eyes distract me even more. "How high are your losses at the gambling hall?"

This time, it was the knight who became flustered. I pressed the advantage, raining blows down on him. One strike slipped through his guard and landed on his shoulder.

"How did you hear about that?" His voice was tight, his grip on his sword even tighter.

"I have friends in low places, if you recall." My chuckle quickly turned into a grunt as I parried his blade. "I assume that was the reason your advancement came at a good time."

"I would kindly request that you keep your nose out of my personal affairs, *Orion.*" His tightly-controlled swings belied his agitation.

"Contrary to what you seem to believe, I did not go seeking that information out in some attempt at blackmail." I parried his next strike and forced him back with a few thrusts.

"Is that so?" Doubt and sarcasm dripped from his voice.

"It is. If you were going to spill my secrets, you would have done so by now. But you did not, despite the fact such information could have earned you a reward from my father." The knight glanced at me in surprise, and I took the opportunity to get in a few strikes.

"I suppose I was the one being nosy," Sir Rigel finally admitted. I smiled.

"In all honesty, I have had some...concerns, as of late," I relented, matching his honesty. "I was relieved Nyra was not upset with me for withholding certain information, but I was also disappointed."

"Why is that?" He parried my strike and forced me to guard against a quick succession of jabs.

"The original reason I went to town in disguise, years ago, was to see how the rest of the kingdom lived, and to experience what that would be like for myself," I explained. "To escape the weight of everyone's deference and expectations, if only for a time. But Nyra almost immediately petitioned me to speak of her cause to my father after she found out."

Our swords clashed in silence for a few moments, the thunk of wood hitting wood oddly cathartic.

"I can see how you would value others seeing you for you, and not your title. And how that could tempt someone to ask for favors." The knight frowned, and I appreciated how quick he was to pick up on what I left unsaid.

"Exactly. I do understand why..." I trailed off, trying to find the right words.

"But it leaves a sour taste in your mouth? Makes you question your relationship?" Sir Rigel supplied.

I nodded. My blade rebounded off of his, and I used the momentum to sweep the blade towards his unprotected ribs. The knight danced to the side, and we began to circle once more.

"I have..." I hesitated, debating how much I trusted him. He already knew one of my secrets, and had kept it. Perhaps it was time I tried trusting the people around me more. "I have long worried I would never know for sure whether the woman I loved would love my title instead of me."

Sir Rigel lowered his sword, planting the tip in the packed soil. "I believe you will be able to tell. But if you do have doubts, you can always come to one of your friends for advice." He paused for a moment, but then added, "If you need someone within the castle to listen, then I would be happy to lend an ear."

I lowered my own sword as well, surprised by his insight and offer. I had given a little trust, and received even more in return. I clapped him on the shoulder with a grin. "I just might take you up on that."

"Prince Sterling!" I turned at the sound of Zale's voice. He was walking briskly towards me across the training courtyard with an envelope in his hands. There was only one reason Zale would come find me himself.

"From my father?" I asked as he reached me.

"I was told it was urgent." My attendant handed the message to me, and I quickly tore it open and scanned the contents.

"It would seem we have something to discuss over lunch." My pulse sped up at the vague request for my presence.

Had the king somehow caught wind of my nightly activities? I glanced at Sir Rigel, but he shook his head. It was possible he wanted to inquire about my progress on a cure, or it could be completely unrelated.

"Same time tomorrow?" I looked to the knight.

"Of course, Highness." I tossed him my practice sword, and he bowed respectfully as I strode towards the keep, Zale falling into step beside me.

"Any word from the herbalists we contacted?" I had meant to check earlier, but it had slipped my mind.

"There has been little progress made so far," Zale reported. "And that stack on your desk continues to grow."

"I know," I sighed. "I will work on that after my meeting with my father."

"Then I shall organize them into piles according to urgency."

"I would appreciate it." I nodded my thanks as we parted ways, and made my way to the dining room, where Sir Magnus was diligently standing guard at the door. He inclined his head to me as I entered.

"You sent for me, Father?" I kept my tone even as I took a seat at the table laden with fresh fruits and cheeses. The circles under my father's eyes seemed darker than usual. And was I imagining it, or were there more silver hairs in his beard than there were last week?

"Yes, I wanted to ask how preparations for the Festival are going." He gave me a warm smile before he took a bite of an apple slice. I let out a silent breath, relieved my secret was still safe. For now.

"There were a handful of issues with some of the vendors' permits and some scheduling conflicts, but nothing I could not handle. Overall, everything is proceeding smoothly, and will be ready for next week." Overseeing the preparations had not been nearly as difficult as I had expected. Then again, I was already used to this kind of work because of my guild.

"I am glad to hear it, Sterling." He gave me a nod of approval, and I sat a little straighter in my chair.

"Father, I know I may be asking too much of you, but... Would you consider increasing the number of wishes granted during the Festival?" I asked cautiously.

My father set down his fork on his lunch plate with a *clink*. "There is only so much the amulet can handle."

I nodded, as if this was new information to me. "Would it contain enough starlight to grant an additional 1-3 wishes per night?" Without putting yourself in danger? I added silently.

The king drummed his fingers against the linen tablecloth as he considered. I almost asked if keeping a supply of bottled starlight on hand would make it easier, but restrained myself. He might become suspicious if I appeared to know more than I should.

"Perhaps," he acquiesced, though he did not look particularly thrilled with the idea. Not that I blamed him—granting wishes was incredibly mentally strenuous.

"I only ask because there has been such a surge in the emergency queue." I pursed my lips. Zale had informed me that the council that oversaw those requests was already overwhelmed—but I had a terrible suspicion that it was only going to get worse.

Just in the last few days, Noctus had brought over a dozen plague victims to the guild, all in desperate need of help. Astrid had dropped everything else to focus on creating a cure, with Nova and Castor assisting her. They had yet to identify the cause, but the illness was spreading.

Quickly.

And until we had a cure in hand, the magic of starlight was the only thing we could rely on.

"Hmm. Has there been any progress on a cure?" He looked at me hopefully, but his eyes dimmed when I shook my head.

"I have my best people working on it, though. It is only a matter of time, now." At least, I hoped. And I hoped that time would be sooner, rather than later. If anyone could figure this out, it was Astrid.

I had also asked the court herbalists to take on this task as well. But so far, they had reported little progress. Tomorrow, I would be extending my request to the most reputable apothecaries and herbalists in the city, as well. I planned on offering a generous reward to whomever came up with a cure as additional motivation.

"Good, good," my father murmured, picking up his fork and returning to his meal.

"There was...one other thing about which I would like to inquire," I said slowly. I was not eager to see his reaction, but...I had made a promise, and I was a man of my word.

"Not another request to allow you to use the amulet, I hope?" He laughed, and I cracked a smile that was more like a grimace.

"No, not that. I have actually been contemplating reaching out to the tribes of the Talahari deserts, with the intention of forming an alliance." I held my breath as a charged silence descended.

I watched my father carefully, noting the way his hands trembled as he set his utensils down once more. He dragged his gaze to mine, the sorrow there gutting me to my core.

"I have lost my appetite." The king tossed his napkin on the table and stood up abruptly, the gilded chair nearly falling over with the sudden motion.

"Father, I—" I started, standing up as well. Guilt needled at me.

"You will not speak of them!" He roared with his back to me. "I forbid it!"

Memories of the influx of tribesmen and women in the slums flashed behind my eyes, their gaunt faces and desperate pleas ringing in my ears. The crushing hopes of Nyra and her people weighed on my shoulders, my soul. I needed to do more, both as a guildmaster and a prince. And if that meant dredging up painful memories, so be it. "But we must do *something* about all the refugees!"

Without looking at me, he said in a quieter tone, "Nothing good comes from those people, Sterling. Were it not for their greed and manipulative mind-games, I would have been here when you were born. If I had been *here*, instead of that accursed desert, your mother might still be with us."

A lump rose in my throat, and tears pricked my eyes. "It was not your fault."

His shoulders bowed, my father simply shook his head. "I should have been here." His voice broke on the words, and my heart went out to him. But at the same time, *he* was the one who had taught me that I would have to put the kingdom's needs before my own.

Before I could even try to formulate a reply, he had swept out of the room. I slowly sank down into my chair, and propped my elbows on the table with my head in my hands. An incredibly un-princely thing to do, but I was beyond caring.

I never meant to hurt him, and I had never seen him lose his composure like that before. I supposed that just signified how deeply he had loved my mother.

Oh, what I would not give to have had the chance to meet her. But even if it were possible, such magic would be forbidden. My father and I would both have to console ourselves with the thought that she watched over us from above.

Sitting here and feeling bad for myself was not helping. I got up from the depressingly-empty table and strode back to my rooms, intent on changing into my commoner's garb. I passed a patrolling Sir Rigel on my way out of the castle, and chuckled at the way he scowled when I winked at him.

Hopefully, he would cover for me if anyone noticed my absence. I grimaced. Then again, after that debacle in the dining room, I doubted that was even a possibility.

I may have hit a wall as Prince Sterling, but as Orion, there was still more I could do.

I loved the feeling of freedom, of anonymity that came with leaving the castle behind. I loved the smell of roasting meat and baking bread that wafted from the taverns and inns, and the sights and sounds of little children running through the streets, happily laughing as they played one last game of shooting stars before it was time for dinner.

The setting sun gilded the ordinarily drab buildings and cobblestones, painting them into roads of gold. Pride swelled in my chest as I secretly watched my people finishing up their chores and duties for the day, their heads held high as they returned to their homes and families for the evening meal.

Every one of them was united by a strong desire to work hard, to give their children a better world to inherit than the one they had been handed. And although some certainly waited on a wish to make their dreams come true, many others built their dreams themselves, brick-by-brick and day-by-day.

They made me want to be better, to be a prince they could be proud of—one they could trust and depend upon. Even if they did not know it yet.

I strolled along the streets, the sound of my steps lost in the bustle around me. Beneath the hood of my cloak, I kept my eyes peeled, constantly roving for anything amiss, and my ears attentive to even the slightest cough. Noctus had been working extra hard as of late, to find plague victims we could aid. It seemed only right that I join in the search as well.

I moved through the merchant district, frowning when I began to notice more and more tribesmen and women skulking about in the shadowy alleys, looks of envy or hatred on many of their faces. The Astorians tended to shy away from them all with equal measure, though a decent number still dropped spare coins into the bowls of those who were begging.

It struck me, then. Of all the people who had been stricken by the plague, not one had been from the desert. If they were somehow immune...perhaps if Astrid could find the reason why the immigrants were unaffected, it might help her develop a cure for my people.

I had made no plans to meet with Nyra tonight, but I had no time to lose. Perhaps she might have an idea of what kept her people so healthy. My ears grew warm. Plus, after the day I had had...spending some time with her would be nice.

I wandered from tavern to tavern, checking her usual haunts. She had taken my advice to perform her tribe's dances in various squares and taverns, since sharing her story that way would win more hearts to her cause than words alone. I stopped to chat with Ace for a few minutes, but she was nowhere to be found.

Finally, as twilight gave way to night and the stars winked to life, I heard a familiar drum beat when I poked my head into a tavern I had rarely visited before on my rumor-gathering missions. And sure enough, I found Nyra dancing to the music, her hips swaying and golden ornamental discs tinkling with a music all their own.

But this time, she was not alone.

A tall tribesman danced at her side, also clad in their traditional dress. His clothes were dyed the same bright red as hers, though there were far fewer adornments. His vest was sleeveless, with only a handful of buttons running down the center, which glinted gold in the candlelight.

But it was the way he was touching her, looking at her that set my blood boiling. I stalked through the patrons who had crowded round to watch, many of whom hurried out of the way when they saw the expression on my face. I tried to ignore the deafening doubts that roared through my mind with little success.

Was this why Nyra was dancing in a tavern far removed from where I usually spent my time? How did she know this male? And was it my imagination, or did his hands linger longer than necessary every time he touched her waist to guide her steps?

I folded my arms across my chest.

I knew the moment Nyra spotted me. She missed a step, stumbling, and the tribesman turned to glare at me. I glared right back. It was the same tribesman who had glared at me in the market square, the one who had threatened me when I took Cosmo's star pendant back. He took every opportunity to shoot dark looks my way, even as Nyra kept glancing worriedly between us. All too soon and not soon enough, the song came to an end, and Nyra hurriedly made her way to me, her chest heaving.

"Pri—" she faltered at my glower. "I mean, Orion, what are you doing here?"

"I could ask you the same," I bit out as the tribesman hurried to her side, his stance telling me he was prepared to fight. "Who is this?" I jerked my chin at the male, who bristled.

"That—this is Tariq. My cousin," Nyra rushed to say, still sounding breathless. I was almost surprised he had not used a false name to peddle his phony cure.

Only because I was looking for it did I notice the way Tariq's jaw clenched, as if he wanted to disagree, but knew better than to contradict her. Though I could count only my father as a blood relative, I was fairly certain family members did not look at each other the way Tariq had been looking at Nyra.

"What a pleasant surprise to see you tonight." Nyra looped her arm through mine when I did not answer, and began tugging me towards the bar. "I thought you would not be able to meet again until our date at the Festival."

I felt my anger and confusion softening at her gentle touch, but my voice was still gruff as I said, "I...needed to get away."

We both sat, but I did not take my eyes off of her as she ordered drinks for the both of us. When they came, she looked down and fiddled with her tankard, instead of drinking it.

"I understand. Being responsible for others is a heavy load to bear." Did I imagine the way her eyes darkened? "My tribe, the Akangli, were the first to have our oasis shrink to practically nothing. I never want to have to watch someone die over a sip of water, ever again."

After a moment, I said, "I admire how deeply you care for your people, and how dedicated you are to finding a solution for them. Even if I disagree with your methods."

She finally looked up, and I was rewarded with a slight smile. "I do appreciate your advice—you were right. Astorians are much more inclined to listen if I first offer to share my people's dances with them."

I nodded with a smile, finally relaxing.

Nyra dropped her voice to a whisper as she leaned closer, and I saw Tariq shift uncomfortably out of the corner of my eye. "Have you...have you had a chance to ask your father about my request?"

She looked up at me through her thick eyelashes, and my mood soured. "I did bring it up, but..." I sighed, grimacing as I remembered the look on my father's face.

"But?" Her brows creased.

"It will take some time for him to come around." I skirted the issue, hoping my words would eventually be proven true. I hated the way her face fell at the news. "The subject of the desertlands do not bring up positive memories for him. However, I will keep trying, for as long as it takes."

I placed my hand over hers comfortingly, but her gaze fell nonetheless. She closed her eyes, as if in pain.

"I may not have much time left." The words were whispered, barely audible over the din of the tavern. Her gaze slowly lifted to mine, the look in their dark and mesmerizing depths pinning me in place. "Those orphans, all the rumors about you..." Her eyes sharpened. "You can grant wishes, too."

I glanced around nervously, hoping no one had overheard. My gut twisted, not liking where this was going. "Are you trying to blow my cover?!"

"You can grant my wish. *You* can restore the oases in the desert!" Her eyes widened with a hope and fervor that made me beyond uncomfortable. I was accustomed to others pinning their hopes on me, but the survival of an entire population was something else entirely.

"As I told you before, I have no idea if that kind of large-scale geographical alteration is even feasible, let alone sustainable! The price for that sort of magic...it may be more than one person can even give!" I hissed.

Nyra blinked. "There is a price for granting wishes?" Her lips twisted in anger. "What you give freely to your own people you would ask me to pay for?" She pulled her hand away.

I grabbed hold of it before she could stand. "No, that is *not* what I said. Nyra, *all* magic has a cost. Does not your mirage magic take a significant amount of your energy and focus? Are you not exhausted after using it for too long, or on too grand a scale?"

"It does," she said slowly, as understanding slowly dawned in her eyes.

"It is the same with the magic of the stars. The wielder must *always* pay a price. If they cannot, if they do not have enough energy and starlight, the magic will take their life-force instead." My hand tightened over hers, and I fought back the familiar lump that rose in my throat. "Just like what happened to my mother."

Nyra's eyes softened, and she laid her free hand on top of mine, her drink all but forgotten. "I had no idea." The words were soft, sad.

I met her gaze, and saw my own sorrow reflected there. She was no stranger to great loss, either. "She died, trying to grant a wish when she was already exhausted. That is why only so many wishes can be granted at a time, even though we would like to grant more."

"The Wish Festivals," she murmured, understanding dawning in the ebony depths of her eyes.

I nodded, then cleared my throat. "I have a proposal for you."

Heat flared in her eyes, and her cheeks flushed a pretty pink. Her dark eyes melted into endless galaxies, flecked with silver stars, and I suddenly realized my misstep.

"A proposal?" she purred.

I swallowed.

"A deal. I meant, a deal." Was I imagining it, or did she look disappointed? "I will continue bringing up your request with my father while researching the possibility of such a monumental wish. If there are precedents in the royal archives, I will find them."

"And in exchange?" Her tone was wary, hopeful.

"In exchange, you will help me find a cure for this plague. After all, with so many people desperately needing their wishes granted to survive the illness, neither my father nor I would have either the power or the time to attempt to grant a wish as grand as yours. I have noticed no one from the desert has contracted the plague, so perhaps your people are immune. If we could find out why, perhaps we could create a cure that is independent of magic entirely."

Nyra shifted uncomfortably, pursing her lips, and glanced at Tariq, who was waiting with the other tribeswomen towards the back. A hint of unease wriggled through me. Was this not an ideal solution for the both of us? But then she smiled, and I pushed my concerns to the back of my mind. She leaned forward and lightly pressed her lips to mine. I grinned, feeling foolish for my earlier worries.

"You have yourself a deal, my prince."

16

Orion

"I have given a great deal of thought to your suggestions," my father said slowly, steepling his fingers. After how our conversation had ended last time, I was surprised to receive another summons from him so soon.

"And...?" I prompted when he fell silent. I tried to keep my gaze from straying to Mother's portrait.

"I have decided to heed your advice, and increase the number of wishes granted each night of the festival from three to five, in addition to granting emergency wishes weekly instead of twice a month."

"Thank you, Father. The people will be overjoyed to hear this," I said warmly. I hoped this response, small though it may seem, would reassure the people that their king was not blind to their troubles. Such actions would speak far louder than words.

"I am sure they will be," the king said with a sigh. "People are always happy when they get what they desire, regardless of what it costs *me*. It is when they do not that I become the villain instead of the hero in their eyes."

I sobered at his words. I stood and walked around the desk to rest my hand on his shoulder, which had borne the weight of the entire kingdom alone for so long.

"We never wanted people to become dependent on wishes, but it is too late to change that now." He sighed heavily, rubbing his brow. I hated seeing him so...despondent.

"You have made such an incredible difference in so many of our people's lives. I know none of this has been easy for you," I said around the sudden lump in my throat. My gaze found the painting, as did his. "And I think Mother would have been proud of all you have accomplished."

He laid his hand over mine. His callouses had faded over time, but they were still the strong, capable hands they had always been. Our emotions hovered in the air, a heady combination of love and loss, tempered by a tired determination. My father's strength of character inspired me. It always had.

"I sure hope so." He cleared his throat. "I also wanted to...apologize for how I spoke to you before. I should not have raised my voice."

"No apology is necessary, Father. I know it is a difficult subject for you." I patted his shoulder as I returned to my seat, trying to work up the nerve for my next request. "I never meant to cause you pain—I simply wanted to understand."

His eyes softened, the dancing firelight gilding his dark hair. "What is it you want to know, son?"

"I understand why alliance talks with the tribes fell through initially, but...why were they never resumed?" Sure enough, his expression hardened for a moment before he sighed heavily.

"My efforts to re-establish ties with those barbarians were never successful. There was always some new excuse, whether it be the weather or the timing. But I had my suspicions." He scowled.

I blinked. "You mean to say it was the *tribesmen* that refused to form an alliance, despite their worsening predicament?"

"I believe some of the chieftains resented me for rushing home when...when I received the news of your birth, and your mother's...passing," my father said haltingly. "The tribesmen believed that *nothing* was more important than conducting business or religious ceremonies, including their women and children. When I left, they saw me as weak, and therefore, untrustworthy."

When Nyra had bemoaned her people's plight, not once had she mentioned the attempts Astoria had made to form ties. She had made it sound as if her people had been abandoned, when in truth, they had purposefully closed themselves off out of pride. Was she simply unaware of this?

"I wonder if the new Woman-King would be more open to an alliance than her male predecessors," I mused. If she had overthrown the previous chieftains, surely she would have had her own reasons. But perhaps those reasons had something to do with the way their men treated their women. And if that were the case, she might not have an unfavorable opinion of a man who would drop everything for his family.

"Hmm. It may be worth considering." A thoughtful look crossed my father's face, and I decided to leave the subject alone for now. It was enough that he was open to the idea of reaching out one last time.

And Nyra would be happy to hear of this progress.

If Astoria could ally with the Woman King and the tribes of the Talahari Desertlands, we could open up new lines of trade and defend each other from the incursions of the witches. An alliance could give the Kingdom of Harland and the Sylvaine Druidlands pause, and a greater reason for them to ally with us, or at least cease their probing of our borders.

And if I were able to broker this alliance, then I might be able to finally convince my father to let me help him with wish-granting—in an official capacity. All parties stood to benefit, if this was handled correctly. Not to mention how happy it would make Nyra.

To secure an alliance with the tribes, we would have to provide a resolution to their problem; But did the amulet have enough power to fundamentally alter the geography of the desert in such a way? As far as I knew, such a feat had never been attempted, and my forays into the archives had only confirmed that suspicion.

"Is the amulet capable of restoring the oases in the desert?" I asked aloud. If anyone knew the answer, it would be my father.

"Hmm. Were your mother here, I could say yes with confidence. But without a fallen star wielding the magic...I do not believe it is possible." He grew very still, his eyes boring into mine. "You were not thinking of trying to grant a wish to restore them, were you?"

"Fret not, for I am not quite that foolish," I replied, and his shoulders sagged in relief. "What of summoning a rainstorm?"

If renewing the oases was beyond the power of our wish magic, making frequent wishes for rain was a more viable option. That, combined with the opening of trade routes between us, could buy the tribes the time they needed to invent a more permanent solution. One that hopefully had nothing to do with starlight *or* the wicked witches.

"That would be more realistic," he murmured, stroking his beard thoughtfully. "I *have* summoned rain once before, so I know it to be possible. It was quite draining, however, even to summon it from existing clouds. It would be far more difficult to create water-laden clouds where none existed before."

"Difficult, but not impossible?" Hope and unease rose side-by-side. It would be quite the undertaking, but granting this particular wish could solve the tribes' immediate problem. Once Nyra and her people were no longer wholly consumed with their own survival, they could lend their efforts to finding a cure for the plague and a solution to their water crisis.

It was by no means a perfect solution, but it was far better than nothing. At least it was a step in the right direction, for all parties.

"Not impossible," the king conceded, dipping his head in confirmation. "Though I cannot say I would be thrilled to expend so much effort on those proud desert fools."

"If they have a cure for this plague, it may well be worth it. Plus, the witches may think twice before harassing either of our countries if we were fast allies."

My father fell silent for a time, and I was content to let him ruminate on the idea. It was no light matter. I refrained from offering to summon the rainstorms myself, for fear that I would undo all the progress we had made thus far.

"When did you become such a fine prince?" His voice was rough with emotion.

"I have simply had a most wondrous example to model." My smile wobbled at the unexpected praise.

"After the Wish Festival, I have something I want to give you. An early birthday gift of sorts, from me—and your mother." His smile was tinged with sorrow.

My birthday had always been a bittersweet occasion for the both of us. It marked the day when he had gained a son but lost his queen. But he always put on a brave face, for my sake. "Then I will do everything in my power to ensure that the festival goes perfectly, so we can celebrate properly afterwards."

17

Astrid

"You promised Estelle, Nova and Castor that you would take them to the Wish Festival." I had been looking forward to attending with Orion and the others for weeks.

"I know." Orion sighed wearily, and ran a hand through his dark hair. He leaned casually against the doorframe of my workshop. "I was looking forward to it too. Something has...come up. But I will make a valiant attempt to join everyone for part of the night market."

I frowned. Orion had always been able to spend at least two or three days of the festival with us in the past, likely because King Cedric was the one who performed the ceremonies. Did that mean the prince was now more involved with planning the festival this year?

Would he be giving the same sorry excuse to Nyra? Or was that *tribeswoman* the reason for his upcoming absence?

Jealousy prickled under my skin like thorny vines, scratching at my heart. What did he see in that woman? And how had he become so completely enamored with her so quickly, when he was still so stand-offish even with the people who owed him everything?

"Will you be the one granting wishes during the Festival?" I crossed my arms over my chest.

"No," Orion hedged after a lengthy pause.

When he failed to elaborate, I bit out, "It would be nice if you trusted us as much as we trust you." I swallowed. "If you had trusted *me* enough to tell me the truth."

And there it was: the real reason I was angry. I had always known Orion was not his real name, that there were things he kept from me. I had decided long ago that it did not matter to me who he really was, because I knew who he was on the inside. The fact that he was a prince did not change that fact. But I was angry, and I was hurt that the only reason he had told me was because he had to, and not because he wanted to. Not because he trusted me.

Orion looked at me with surprised wariness. But then he looked away, and I resigned myself to whatever lie he was about to spin with that silver tongue of his. It was always like this.

"I...you are right." I blinked. "I find myself being both too trusting and not trusting enough."

"Why?" I took a step closer, shocked Orion had admitted it.

"Suffice it to say, the boy I considered my closest friend had been sent by my father's enemies, to use me against him," Orion said darkly.

I put my hand on his arm, so he would look at me. I chose my next words very carefully. "Everyone in this guild would lay down their lives for you."

Orion's startled blue eyes met mine.

"You saved each of us, in one way or another. There is nothing any one of us wants from you, other than your presence. Quite the contrary—we want to do whatever we can to help you. To do for others what you have done for us." I hoped he felt the sincerity in my words, in my eyes.

"I...truly?" For the first time since I had met him, Orion seemed to be at a loss for words.

"There is nothing I would not do for you." I felt vulnerable, saying my thoughts out loud. But the tender look in his eyes made the risk worth it.

"Thank you. For being honest with me." Orion's voice had dropped an octave, the smooth velvet sending shivers down my spine.

"And you with me," I whispered. It was not the whole truth, or the apology I wanted, but it was a start.

The expression on Orion's face lingered in my mind long after he had left the guild house. Even as I set to work preparing dinner for everyone and then later concocting a remedy Nova and Castor thought might have some effect on the plague, thoughts of Orion kept resurfacing. And as much as I hated to admit it, the exotic herbs and spices he had received from Nyra were proving to be more effective in fighting the plague than any of the native ones. I still had yet to concoct a remedy that could cure the sickness, but at least I was finally making significant progress.

A sudden commotion drew me from my thoughts, and I jumped up to investigate. I ran down the hall, only to nearly collide with Noctus.

"Is Orion here?" he asked before I could get a word out.

"No, he left a while ago."

Noctus scowled. "Get your medicine bag. I have a family of four that will not last through the night. I will send a starnote to Orion with the location."

He whipped out his starsteel pocket watch as I ran back to my work table. I donned my cloak and slung my satchel over my shoulder, stuffing the remedies I had been working on into it on a whim. I also added my small bottle of starlight, but between four people, I doubted it would be much help.

I joined Noctus at the door, and we raced into the night. The cobblestone streets were deserted at this hour, the lampposts doing little to dispel the darkness. I followed Noctus' lead, and I was soon panting as we entered a quiet neighborhood.

It had already been a long day, a long week and month, but I willed my leaden legs to pump faster. I did not have the luxury of being tired and weak. Not when I could save even one more life.

We ran around the back of a modest wooden home, and entered through the kitchen door. The interior smelled musty, and I resisted the urge to cover my nose. We found both parents and two young children huddled together in one large bed in the back room. Thin blankets were heaped on top of them all to ward off the chill.

But based on the dark bruising on their skin and their shallow breathing, they did not have long. They must have been stricken with the plague at least a week ago. It was a miracle all four were still alive.

I immediately set to work, pulling out every remedy I had brought and laying them out on a small chest. I had to buy them time until Orion arrived.

"What can I do?" Noctus asked.

"Get a fire going, and bring me every blanket you can."

As Noctus rushed to do as I requested, I uncorked a vial of one of the remedies Nova and Castor had helped me concoct. I carefully helped the two children sit up and drink half the remedy each. Then I did the same for the two adults.

Not long after taking that, all of their breathing seemed to ease, but only for a time. I gave them each what remedies I could, but nothing else seemed to have much of an effect. Their breathing was becoming labored again, and I was running out of tasks to give Noctus to keep him from hovering.

"How much longer?" I murmured, pulling him aside. It had already been over an hour since we had arrived.

"Not long. He is on his way." But Noctus seemed uncertain, as if even he was wondering what was taking him so long.

"He might be lost. Go and guide him here." Noctus nodded, and did as I asked.

If only I could use my magic to enhance the effectiveness of my remedies... But using even a tiny amount of wild magic would reactivate the curse.

I could not do it. Our mothers' sacrifices would not be in vain—no matter how guilty I felt for not doing everything I could for these people, even as they wasted away in front of me.

I wiped the sweat from my brow, willing my tired eyes to stay open. I refused to give up until the end. I just had to hope Orion would arrive in time.

18

Orion

"You only just returned, and now you must leave again?" Zale questioned exasperatedly. "What about all of this paperwork?"

"Emergencies will not bend to my schedule, unfortunately," I said as I settled my cloak over my shoulders. It was a good thing I had yet to return the amulet to its pedestal—according to the starnote, I would need to use most of its starlight reserves tonight.

"What, exactly, is this emergency that cannot wait?" Zale crossed his arms.

"A friend needs my help." Then an idea struck me. "Have you seen Sir Rigel today, by chance?"

Zale raised an eyebrow at the change of subject. "Now that you mention it, I do not believe I have. It must be his day off today."

I cursed under my breath. In a short time, I had already come to rely on the knight to cover for me, on the nights I wore a different name. Perhaps this time, I would ask Zale.

"Lock the door to my study. If anyone asks, Zale, tell them I am busy preparing for the festival, and not to be disturbed. Please," I added. "I would not ask if it were not important."

I met his gaze, knowing I was asking him to lie for me, and that half-hearted excuses would get me nowhere.

Finally, he nodded. "Fine. But you owe me a drink—and an explanation, Highness."

"Thank you, Zale. You will get both—soon," I promised as I walked out the door. I resisted the urge to run, knowing that would draw far too much attention. It had taken me far longer than I had anticipated to tear myself away from that council meeting and stop by my study.

I pulled out my watch and glanced once more at the faintly-glowing letters on the starsteel. It was an address in an unfamiliar neighborhood, so I had better get moving. I left the castle grounds by vaulting over a low section of the wall, and began jogging towards where I thought the neighborhood was located.

I wasted precious minutes peering at houses, searching for the right one. I tried not to take the dense cloud cover as an ominous sign. As I worked my way down another street, I saw a shadowy figure running towards me. I reached for my sword before I recognized Noctus.

"This way, quick!" Noctus turned on his heel, and I followed where he led.

He brought me to a small, wooden house, and the intense smell of mold and mildew hit me as soon as we entered. A short walk down the hallway revealed a family of four lying beneath a small mountain of blankets, with Astrid hovering over them. Based on their bruised skin and labored breathing, they did not have long.

I had never seen Astrid so exhausted. Wisps of hair had escaped her braid, and the dark circles under her eyes were stark in her too-pale face. A line of empty glass vials and jars marched in a line on top of a storage chest. She looked up from adding another empty jar to the line-up when I entered, and looked to be clutching another small bottle in one hand.

"Took you long enough," Astrid mumbled, before she collapsed into the room's sole chair and closed her eyes. She went to sleep almost instantly.

"Orion, there is a commotion over at Ace's Tavern with some tribesmen. I will take care of it—you focus on them," Noctus said as he snapped his watch closed.

"I would appreciate it." At least now I would not need an excuse to get him to leave the room while I granted these peoples' wishes.

Noctus left just as quietly as he came. I hesitated, my gaze falling on Astrid, but then I closed the door. I did not have time to move her, and she was unlikely to wake anytime soon. Though, even if she did, I could trust her. Right?

I approached the family, and was relieved to see that all four were still breathing, however faintly. The father was wheezing and the mother coughed faintly, but the two children were limp. Had I arrived much later, it would have been too late.

"There is little time. Repeat after me: I wish for myself, my wife and my two children beside me to be made well and remain so."

The man had to clear his throat three times before he managed to say the words, so I used that time to begin pulling the starlight magic from the amulet. The moment the man finished speaking his wish, I shut my eyes and brought my will to bear on the magic.

Thanks to the dense cloud cover tonight, there was little starlight to draw from the air. So I pulled and pulled at the amulet, taking more and more from the star sapphire, until the very air came alive with soft, silvery light. I directed the magic to seep into the four figures in front of me, one at a time, to burn away the sickness within them.

I started with the father, and the bruising on his skin began to fade as the starlight did its work. Once his breathing evened out and nothing malignant remained, I left a tiny kernel of magic there, to prevent him from contracting the plague again. Then I moved on to the mother, following the same process until she was well. I heard her begin to quietly weep as I turned my attention to the children.

I could feel the magic in the amulet thinning, and I sent a quick prayer to the stars that it would be enough to save the lives before me. I had to be more careful with the first child, to control the wild magic as my mind ached from the strain and my back began to burn.

I was panting by the time the first child was healed. There was so little magic left that I feared it would not be enough. But I had to try. Even if I could not heal her fully, perhaps I could buy her some time until the amulet regained its magic.

I poured every wisp of starlight I could muster into the little girl, so the silver light could cleanse the sickness. I was only part way through when the magic ran dry, the flow of magic slowing to a trickle, until it stopped completely. The amulet was completely drained of its starlight.

I felt my heart sink. What was I meant to tell her family? With the amount of magic that had been left, I had only managed to buy the girl a few more hours. The plague would soon undo the work of the starlight, but I doubted the amulet would be restored enough in those few hours to make a significant difference.

How had my father withstood the horrible choice that now lay before me? If I did use some of my lifeforce to grant this wish, would it take the entirety of it? Or would it simply shave off a handful of months, or even years?

I grit my teeth, torn by the very decision I had hoped I would never have to make. It was easy to declare I would never make my mother's mistake, but quite another to turn away from the dying girl right in front of me.

I heard a quiet thud behind me, the sound of glass hitting the floor. By some miracle, I felt a sudden influx of starlight suddenly suffuse the air. Before it could dissipate, I grabbed hold of it, using it to power the rest of the wish. A few moments was all I needed to finish cleansing the girl, and to leave a miniscule kernel of starlight within her.

I opened my eyes to see all four of them sobbing as they held each other close, their skin practically glowing with health. A wave of dizziness hit me, and I staggered over to the wall. I leaned against it, then slid down to the floor next to the still-sleeping Astrid. It was then I noticed that the bottle Astrid had been clutching now lay on its side at her feet, a few wisps of starlight still lingering inside.

I let out a breath. So Astrid was the reason I had been able to save the girl, without resorting to sacrificing myself. She had saved me from that agony of indecision, from that impossible choice. On a whim, I pressed a light kiss to the back of her limp hand. I would have to remember to thank her properly, later.

"Thank you, Orion," the mother cried as she tucked her daughter's head beneath her chin. The sight made my heart swell. The little girl would never have to know the pain of losing her mother, as I had.

"We will never forget what you have done for us. If there is any way we can repay you..." the father trailed off as he choked up. He kept running his hands over his boy's arms, as if he could hardly believe he was alive. "And I swear, me and mine shall never reveal what transpired here."

I nodded my head, too exhausted to even speak. I leaned my head back against the wall. I needed to close my eyes, just for a moment...

"Orion, wake up!" It was the fear in Noctus' voice that had me blinking my sticky eyes open. Noctus was never afraid.

"What is it?" I glanced to the side. Astrid was still asleep in the chair, but the family of four was no longer in the bed. Instead, there was one man, sprawled across it.

"Sir Rigel, the castle Knight Commander." Noctus pointed at the figure on the bed, and my gaze sharpened on the red staining his normally immaculate hands. "He was stabbed."

I lurched to my feet and staggered over to the bed as another wave of dizziness hit me. Blood bloomed from a wound in his stomach, staining his tunic crimson. His eyes were clenched shut, and he was gritting his teeth against the pain.

"How?" I rasped. We had sparred only yesterday!

"He racked up a huge debt from gambling. A tribesman came to collect, and when Rigel refused to hand over his wish pendant..." Noctus grimaced. "I only arrived afterwards."

"It was my own damn fault," Rigel rasped, cracking one eye open to look at me. He reached one shaking hand up, and I clasped it in both of mine. "I was a fool."

"You got that right. What kind of knight loses at poker?" I tightened my grip.

"At least…" He coughed, a horrible, wet sound. "At least I am not alone…at the end."

I stared down at the friend who had been like an older brother to me as he fell unconscious, his hand going limp and his breathing became more ragged. Gut wounds, as a rule, were generally fatal. But I had already exhausted the amulet's power. It would be *days* before it recuperated enough power to heal something like this.

Rigel did not have days.

He had *minutes*.

I felt something in me snap.

"Get me starlight," I said without looking up.

"Starlight?" Noctus parroted, bewildered.

"I need bottled starlight. I care not how you get it." I snapped my gaze to his. "From a shop or even straight off a starship."

Noctus nodded once, twice. "Understood."

He ran from the room. As I closed the door behind him, I caught a glimpse of the four I had already saved tonight, sitting around their kitchen. Love and hope shone in their eyes. The exact opposite of how I felt.

I locked it.

I removed my cloak, cast it aside. I tore off my own tunic and ripped it into strips. I balled some of it up, ripped open Rigel's tunic so I could see the wound, and packed the extra fabric in to stanch the flow. I needed to buy some time.

I doubted Noctus would be able to find any starlight. It was late; most shops had closed long ago. I had not had a chance to replenish the depleted stores I normally kept at the guild. I had mostly made the request to get Noctus out of the room. But then I wondered—would Astrid have some?

I glanced at the bottle that still lay on the floor, and picked it up carefully. There was still a little starlight trapped inside, a glimmer of magic that called to me. It was not nearly enough for a wish of this magnitude.

I rummaged through her satchel, and found a collection of herbs and remedies, but no more starlight. I would have to use the few wisps that were left in this bottle, and use my own life for the rest.

And here I had thought I would escape this night unscathed.

Hope was a cruel thing, indeed.

I had vowed to myself long ago that this was the one line I would never cross. That I would never make my mother's mistake, and that I would never abandon my father, as she had abandoned us.

But for the first time, I thought I understood a fraction of what must have been going through her mind, how she was tormented by the knowledge that she alone had the power to save the life that was before her, and that to turn away would eat at her soul just as surely as the magic would. Was this paralyzing combination of fear and determination what my mother had felt, when she sacrificed her life for a stranger's?

I would never forgive myself if I let Rigel die right in front of me.

I pulled at the last dregs of magic in the star sapphire. For a moment, I felt it respond, felt a stirring of its magic. But then it fizzled out and died, completely spent.

I let out a breath. I just had to hope the cost to my life would be something I could pay. My father's sorrowful face flashed in my mind, but I pushed it aside. Perhaps there was a way to lessen the cost.

Instead of releasing the starlight into the air as I normally would, I upended the bottle against my skin. If I could channel it through my body, with the starsteel of the pendant to amplify it, perhaps the cost to me would be somewhat lessened.

I closed my eyes and sighed as the cool starlight touched my skin, calming my raging headache. I pulled the starlight in, guiding it through my core so I could add my own lifeforce to the magic. I put my hand over Rigel's wound, and did what I had never done before. What I swore I never would.

I made a wish.

"I wish for Rigel Gallahad to be made healthy and whole."

For a moment, everything went silent, as if the stars held their breath. And then, they began to sing.

I sucked in a breath as the starlight within me began to expand, swirling and growing stronger with every passing moment. I marveled at the power of the silver light, at the symphony it wove. It grew until it pressed against my skin, a wild, living thing that refused to be contained. It writhed out of my control, a few wisps escaping into the air.

Rigel moaned.

I refocused. I had no idea where all of this magic had come from, or why the stars had answered my call. Why, instead of leeching away my lifeforce, it was bolstering it. But I was not about to let it go to waste.

I channeled the magic through my arm and into my hand, let it flow from my fingertips like a silver rain. I felt connected to the magic in a way I never had before, and even after it sank into Rigel's skin, it waited for my command.

I gave it.

Within seconds, the fatal wound was gone. I opened my eyes to watch in awe as his skin knit back together, until not even a scar remained. I waved my hand over the knight, and the starlight found and fixed every other little scrape and bruise that was on him. His sallow skin soon gleamed with health, and his breathing deepened in peaceful sleep.

A point on my back turned to ice, in contrast to the usual burning sensation I always experienced. Normally, whenever I used the amulet to grant a wish, I always felt drained and exhausted afterwards. But after both making and granting a wish, I felt like I could dance through the sky. Instead of fading away, the magic lingered in my body, waves of comforting coolness singing through my veins.

What had I just done?

And more importantly, could I do it again?

19

Astrid

It was the flickering silver light that woke me. I blinked open my tired eyes, resisting the urge to groan at the way the uncomfortable wooden chair was digging into my ribs. I was still in the house of mildew, where I had been tending to the plague-stricken family.

I stared in confusion at the sight that met my eyes. Across from me, instead of that family, Orion was tending to a different man, who looked vaguely familiar. I squinted at him, noting the horrendous wound in his side and the shiny boots on his feet. The standard-issue boots that castle knights wore. And then I remembered, as I peered at his too-pale face; This was the man Orion had revealed himself to, the day we defeated Khalifon once and for all.

What was his name again?

He was the castle's Knight Commander.

The light that had woken me caught my attention again, and I felt my cheeks flame when I realized Orion was tunicless, with his back towards me. But any self-consciousness I felt quickly faded. I stared in awe at the galaxy of glowing stars that was inked in starlight across his broad back. Each individual star glimmered in the dim light, winking with every movement he made.

Some of the stars were clustered, as if in a pattern. No, in a constellation! Stretching across his back, I identified Vulpecula, the fox constellation, and Lupus, the wolf constellation, alongside many others. But the largest of the constellations living in his skin was Orion, the archer constellation.

I blinked. Was that why he called himself Orion?

My guild master lifted a necklace in his hand, and I nearly gasped. It was the star sapphire pendant I had only ever seen the king wear during Wish Festivals. He always wore it while granting wishes, and I remembered watching it glow with starlight whenever he did. I had always assumed the necklace was simply a sentimental heirloom, but what if it was something more? What if it was what made wish-granting possible for those who were mere mortals and not true fallen stars?

But unlike the one in my memories, the one in Orion's hand was dull and lifeless.

He clenched it in his fist before letting it drop back to his chest, heaving a sigh. His shoulders slumped for a moment before he squared them, as if he were bracing himself. I held my breath as he held his hand over the gruesome wound in the knight's side and the remains of Orion's tunic, which he must have been using to stanch the flow of blood. Was I finally going to witness one of his miracles?

"I wish for Rigel to be made healthy and whole."

As soon as the words left his lips, every star on his back lit up one-by-one, with a light to rival their counterparts in the night sky. I squinted my eyes against their intense glow, refusing to look away, even for a moment. I would not forsake this opportunity to see how Orion had been granting wishes all this time.

One lone star between his heavily-muscled shoulder blades shone far brighter than the others, which seemed dim in comparison. Starlight streamed from that star into Rigel in a river of rippling, cascading silver. The man's breathing immediately began to ease.

And when Orion moved his head, I saw the midnight-black of his hair change to a bright, glowing silver, with wisps of starlight encircling his head like a halo, or a crown of stars.

I had never seen a more awe-inspiring sight.

As I watched, the knight's wound healed, and his breathing deepened in peaceful sleep. The brightest star on Orion's back flared brilliantly for a moment before winking out entirely, causing him to flinch, as if in pain. But wisps of starlight still floated around Orion and Rigel, filling the room with effervescent light.

Even though the wish had been granted, Orion's stars and hair still glowed silver. He raised his hands in front of him, as if even he was surprised by the faint glow they gave off, the starlight that dripped from his skin.

Orion—no, Prince Sterling—looked for all the world like a fallen star. Like the beings of legend, the ones worshipped so fervently by the druids, and desired so dearly by the witches.

I must have made some small noise, because he suddenly turned around. His glowing, silvery-blue eyes locked on mine, and I could not help the words that slipped past my lips.

"The Starborn Prince."

20

Orion

"Here are the reports from the committees on decorations and stall permits, as well as from the Master of Ceremonies," Zale said as he plopped each stack of paperwork onto my desk.

I stared at the ever-increasing pile. "How has my father been managing to get all of this done in time for every single Wish Festival?"

"He is quite the disciplined and hard-working man." Zale's tone was full of admiration.

"Very true," I said with a chuckle. No one could claim he was not doing his utmost. Well, at least no one who truly knew him. "Have there been any more...incidents?"

Zale's eyes shied away from mine. "Hmm."

"Zale." I glowered. "Just tell me."

He sighed. "There *has* been a report of more fights between tribesmen and those who made ill-begotten bargains with them."

"More false claims and useless potions?"

"I am afraid so, Highness." Zale scowled. "At first, I thought it a great kindness to allow those seeking sanctuary within our borders. But now…now I can plainly see how such kindness has become a great weakness, instead."

"If only there were a surefire solution to their water crisis," I muttered. During my spare moments, in between my time at Hyperion and my duties as a prince, I had been combing the royal library, searching for precedents of any similar large-scale wishes being granted.

So far, the only recorded example I had found that held any relevance was when my mother had once granted a request for rain over the Kingdom of Harland. According to the account, it had been extremely taxing on her, even to summon a rainstorm for two days. My father had seemed open to the idea of summoning rain for them, but if it had been so difficult for a true fallen star, it may prove too great a task for the already taxed amulet she left behind.

Perhaps it would be better to think of a solution that involved creating a new fresh water spring. But I was uncertain if that was even a possibility—if the water supply beneath the desert sands had already been exhausted, was the magic of the stars even powerful enough to create water where none existed?

"Might I recommend devoting your attention to that issue *after* the conclusion of the Wish Festival?" Zale suggested.

"Of course." I balefully eyed the ever-increasing stack of paperwork. "Help me ensure this festival proceeds smoothly, and I will see to it that you receive a generous bonus."

Zale glanced at the stack as well and raised an eyebrow, looking unconvinced.

"And some time off. I have no doubt you could plan quite a few courtship proposals for that lady you always mention with a whole week of free time," I added.

Zale smiled. "It will be the most successful festival to date."

"I appreciate your assistance. Would you check in with the Starburst Committee while I see that the wish selection letters go out today?" The wishes that were to be granted during the festival were always chosen in advance from a pool of requests. That way, the wishers had ample time to memorize the wording of their wish, and there would be no sudden requests for a malicious or overly-vague wish during the ceremony.

"Leave it to me, Highness." Zale bowed before he left to fulfill my requests.

I stretched as I stood, attempting to work out the stiffness in my back. And attempting not to think about the fact that I had yet to have a proper discussion with Astrid, not only about what she had witnessed the other night, but also about my true identity. I dreaded that conversation, but if I were being honest with myself, I was actually quite relieved that she knew my secrets. Now, I no longer had to lie to her.

But I would worry about that later. For now, I had another pressing matter to attend to. I touched the hidden pendant briefly, reassuring myself it was still there, before exiting my study.

"Have you appointed yourself my personal guard, then?" I commented as I began striding through the stone halls, my footsteps muffled by the thick rug underfoot.

"Guarding you is the least I can do," Rigel replied as he fell into step beside me, though he made sure to keep just a pace behind.

I waited until we had passed a pair of guards before I murmured, "You owe me nothing."

"That is all the more reason to give you everything."

I glared at the knight, but he simply smirked at me. Impudent bastard. "You really should still be resting."

"But I have never felt so alive and full of vigor." I rolled my eyes at his enthusiasm. "Resting would be futile."

"If you insist on hovering, I have every intention of putting you to work organizing the Wish Festival with me," I warned him. I was drowning in more work than I knew what to do with, but I had to ensure that everything went perfectly.

"Your wish is my command."

Despite myself, I laughed at the irony. Usually *I* was the one saying that, in so many words. Rigel looked much too pleased with my reaction. But I supposed having him around would not be so bad.

Soon we arrived at the most important room in the keep, whose door was flanked with two of our most skilled knights. There were several identical rooms, all guarded in pairs, but only my father and I knew which room held the precious item at any given time.

"Let no one near while I am inside," I ordered both Rigel and the two knights.

"Understood, Your Highness."

I unlocked and entered the room, locking the door again behind me. It was a simple, circular room, but the walls were painted to look like the night sky. Many of the stars were embedded with tiny mirrors, which reflected the light from the skylight down onto the raised pedestal in the center of the small room.

I withdrew the star sapphire from beneath my garments and returned the precious necklace to its place on the pedestal, nestled securely on a bed of crushed velvet. A glimmer of magic lit the depths of the gem, but it was still far from full strength.

I withdrew a glass vial from my pocket, and carefully uncorked it. I held the pendant steady as I slowly began to pour the liquid starlight onto it. This had been one of my duties for nearly as long as I could remember, to check on the sapphire and ensure it was always filled with starlight. Which was why it had been so easy for me to constantly borrow and return it, with none the wiser.

I tilted the bottle a tad too far, and a drop of starlight fell onto my hand. I felt that silky coolness as it sank into my skin, the buzz of power as it connected with whatever force had awakened in me when I both made and granted a wish to save Rigel's life. The sensation was just as unsettling now as it had been then.

With more caution, I emptied the rest of the bottle into the star sapphire, making sure not to spill another drop. It was imperative that I not overwhelm it with too much starlight at once. Just like soil after a drought, the gem needed time to absorb the starlight properly.

Hopefully, a few cloudless nights combined with the amplifying effects of the mirrors in the walls would fill the sapphire with enough starlight for my father to grant several wishes each night of the festival. But I still planned to check its power levels every day until then. That meant no wish granting for me for the next week, but there was nothing I could do about that.

I corked the empty bottle and returned it to my pocket before opening the door. The two knights flanking the door stared straight ahead, but Rigel turned to greet me. His eyes went wide with alarm, and he quickly strode forward, crowding me back into the room. I frowned at him, and he gestured at me frantically. I closed us back inside the small room.

"What are you doing?" I hissed.

"Your hair and eyes are glowing silver!" Rigel whispered, gesturing towards my face.

"What?" Astrid had mentioned something similar, but I had thought it had just been a trick of the starlight. I walked over to one of the larger mirrors in the room, and my jaw slackened when I saw my reflection.

Was this because of the drop of starlight I had spilled? But this had never happened when I touched starlight before! Unless...

Unless making and then granting my own wish had changed me, somehow.

I fingered a glowing lock of my hair. If my father saw this, he would have many questions that I was not prepared to answer. New worries crowded my mind. Was it only liquid starlight that had this effect on me? Or was it any starlight at all? Could I avoid touching the wisps of starlight that appeared when father granted wishes during the festival? It would be just my luck to accidentally start glowing in front of half the city.

"And now, it is fading." Rigel stared in wonder as the glow slowly faded, and my hair and eyes returned to normal. "Does this always happen?"

"Only since I saved you." I sighed. "Perhaps I should carry a hat with me during the festival."

Rigel looked down, his face tightening.

"It was bound to happen sooner or later. It was only a matter of time before I needed to save someone after I had already spent the magic in the amulet. If anything, I am surprised it did not happen sooner."

Rigel looked away, a muscle in his jaw feathering.

"At least now I have someone by my side who can tell me when it happens. My time as Orion would have been over had

I walked out that door while glowing." I smiled at Rigel, who had finally lifted his gaze from the floor.

"You will never have to fear a sword at your back while I am here," Rigel pledged solemnly. "Or glowing hair."

"Glad to hear it. Now, my faithful knight, you are going to help me tackle that mountain of paperwork. Since I am heading the preparations this time, everything needs to be perfect!"

Before I knew it, the sun had turned the world to gold, and the first night of the Festival was upon us. It had taken much more work than I anticipated, but I had managed to arrange everything in time—with some help.

Both Rigel and Zale had been with me every step of the way. Even now, Rigel refused to let me out of his sight for long. I was becoming accustomed to his reassuring presence.

Once true night had fallen, I stood proudly beside my father, dressed in my regal suit, as the first person stepped forward to make her wish. The middle-aged woman limped slowly through the open town square, which was festooned with floral wreaths and ribbons. Candles flickered on every available surface, in imitation of the glimmering stars above.

The woman ascended the few steps onto the raised dais and knelt before us, and offered her star pendant to my father. He gingerly took the delicate starsteel chain from her, and spoke the ceremonial words.

"Your right as a good subject of Astoria has been recognized. Speak your wish, that it may be heard and granted by the stars." His voice rang out over the gathered crowd, many of whom held festival food in their hands.

"I wish for my twisted leg to be made healthy and whole, now and until I join the stars." Despite the slight tremor in her hands, her voice was steady and true.

"So shall it be," the king responded. Starlight gathered around him, casting him and the woman in silvery light. I made sure not to stand too close. He directed the magic into the woman, concentrating it around her twisted leg, and after only a few moments, it was healed.

She stood up tentatively, and when the leg supported her weight, tears of joy spilled down her cheeks. "Thank you, oh, thank you! Long live King Cedric! Long live the Kingdom of the Stars!"

"Go forth and spread your joy and aid freely, as it has been freely given to you." And with that closing remark, the first wish was complete.

The woman curtsied deeply before descending back into the crowd. Next came a handful of men, women, and children, to make their wishes before their king and countrymen. I was unsurprised that most of the wishes were for health and healing—I *had* pushed for more plague-stricken wishes to be granted, after all.

It was important for the people to see the crown was aware of the plague, and actively offering aid while still searching for a more pragmatic solution. And to fill the void left by Hyperion's absence during the Festival.

Once all of the wishes had been granted for the night, I convened with each of the committees to check that everything was going smoothly. They were, for the most part, but there were still minor hiccups here and there that needed to be addressed. I worked on the solutions in my study till late at night, so I would have them ready to implement by the next morning.

On the second night, my father interspersed the health-related wishes with the kinds of dreams that required no starpower. One young man wished to open his very own bakery, but lacked the resources to do so on his own. Instead of using magic to grant his wish, Father assigned one of the castle bakers to be the boy's mentor, and several clerks to assist him with finding a shop to purchase or lease. In addition, he provided the young man with the funds necessary to open and run the bakery for the first two years.

He was ecstatic with the assistance, as were the others who made a wish that night. And although I saw a handful of tribesmen and women scattered throughout the crowd, there were no disturbances reported beyond the usual disputes that always arose during Festival Week.

The next few nights all went well, and with me pouring an entire bottle of starlight into the star sapphire every day, there was little risk of the pendant running dry—or my father having to supply his own lifeforce to power the magic.

It was on the final night, when I had finally started to relax, that the tribeswomen raised a ruckus.

Just after the third wish of the night had been granted—a mother's plea for her daughter to be cured of her sickness—a group of tribeswomen shoved their way through the crowd. They wore their traditional garments of bright colors and dangling metal ornaments, their cries growing louder as they drew closer to the raised dais.

"When will you grant the rest of the wishes of your people?"

"Before or after the plague takes them all?!"

"Why are some of your subjects more deserving than others?"

The king's royal guards rushed forward to form a wall of shields at the base of the dais, swords and spears sheathed but within easy reach. I stepped in front of my father, my own hand resting on the hilt of my sword as my expression darkened. Rigel readied himself at my side.

I had explicitly told Nyra to warn her people against such displays, as they would only damage the cause of the foreigners. Had Nyra been unable to convince her fellow refugees to abstain from such provocative folly?

My father put a hand on my shoulder, stepping forward to address the crowd as the mood shifted from celebratory to tense. "We are working tirelessly to find a cure for the illness that has been spreading through Astoria. Until one can be created and made available, the emergency queue will double its capacity and frequency."

"That is not nearly enough!"

"More are dying every day!"

"We cannot wait that long!"

The crowd was becoming more agitated, with those closest to the tribeswomen becoming the most distraught. I scanned the crowd with narrowed eyes, seeking to match faces to the loudest voices.

"We have a right to be saved, too!"

At his sharp intake of breath, I glanced at my father's face. I knew that expression. Before I could calm him down, the king bellowed, "Those who came seeking sanctuary and were granted it, who have brought nothing but crime and discontent, have no right to steal the wishes of those who have waited their whole lives!"

Silence descended at his outburst.

"What sort of king leaves his people to suffer and die when he could save them with just a few words?" called a sultry, familiar voice, as one tribeswoman pushed her way to the forefront of the group.

The blood froze in my veins as I locked eyes with Nyra, and she gave me a knowing little smile. Beside me, I felt Rigel stiffen. By the stars, what had gotten into her? Why had she so blatantly ignored my repeated warnings? What did she hope to gain from this? And why was she looking at me like that? Like a cat looks at a mouse?

Could it be...?

Was she about to expose my secret to my father and the entire kingdom?

21

Orion

"Although you freely partake of this country's prosperity, you have yet to learn anything of it. The magic of the stars is *not* an unlimited resource. I am not a fallen star, and I do not have the power to grant hundreds of wishes in an instant. I am a man—a man who continues to try his best to provide for those who chose to live with me in the north." The king's voice strengthened as he regained his composure.

Nyra hesitated. I saw some of the anger melt from the faces of the Astorians in the crowd, though the tribeswomen still scowled.

"Who are you to decide who lives and who dies, whose wishes are more worthy than others?" Nyra tried, changing tact. A few yelled their support and agreement.

"What would you have me do?" Instead of falling for the obvious trap in her words, my father turned it back on her. Nyra startled, seemingly at a loss for words.

"I...I would grant the wish of everyone who cared to make one," she announced boldly.

"And if doing so were not an option? If you could wield only so much magic every night?" he countered. "If the cost of trying to grant so many wishes at once were your own life, or the life of another? Would you do it then?"

Nyra fell silent. Those around her began murmuring amongst themselves. The elders in the crowd nodded along to the king's words, while the youth bore matching looks of surprise and chagrin on their faces.

"You paint me as the villain for not satisfying your demands, ignoring my lifetime's worth of granting wishes in the process. You stir unrest, but offer no solutions of your own. I had been considering extending an offer of alliance and aid to the Talahari Tribes, but if *this* sort of behavior is all I can expect... Then there is little point in sending an envoy to the Desertlands."

Devastation was written across her delicate features. I turned away. I had told her such actions would harm her cause. But had she listened? *No!* What was I meant to say to her later tonight? She had undone all my hard work, and now there was little chance of my father extending aid of any sort to her people.

With her own lips, Nyra had doomed those she sought to save.

"Since you find conditions here so disagreeable, you may return to your homeland. Guards!" At my father's command, the guards waded through the crowd towards Nyra.

I stiffened, resisting the urge to either argue with my father or help her escape. Rigel put a hand on my arm, but he need not have worried. Taking action now would bring too many secrets to light. I had to trust that Nyra was capable of outrunning the guards on her own, this time.

She glanced around frantically, searching for an escape route. She disappeared into the crowd of other brightly-colored tribeswomen, blending in perfectly, just as the guards reached them. They peered at each woman in turn, to find the red and gold one among them.

To my relief, I soon saw a veiled woman in blue slink away from the crowd and into a shadowy side street. None of the guards noticed. It seemed our outing tonight would become a goodbye—if she even stayed long enough for that. A wave of sadness and regret washed over me. It would be far wiser of her to flee Astoria as soon as she was able.

My heart clenched at the thought.

Was that glimpse the last I would ever see of her?

I tapped my heel against the cobblestones as I waited on our designated bench. The night market was in full swing around me, though after the debacle Nyra had caused during the ceremony, the air was far less celebratory than during previous festivals. I hoped Astrid and the rest of the guild were still able to enjoy it, even though I had been unable to join them.

Slipping away had not been difficult, as my father had retired to his study immediately following the conclusion of the ceremony, no doubt to gaze upon Mother's portrait. He had managed to grant the final two wishes of the festival, so at least it had not ended on a sour note. It appeared we would be saving the review meeting for tomorrow, once Father had recovered.

I was dressed in commoner's garb once more, and looked no different from the rest of the festival-goers. I had learned long ago that people would not recognize me when I was not where a prince was expected to be.

The bells tolled the hour, and I counted eleven chimes before they went silent once more. I sighed. Nyra was not coming. Perhaps *I* was the fool for expecting her to still be here, when she should be on her way to the border instead.

I stood. Perhaps I would see if I could watch the starbursts with Estelle and the rest of the guild.

"Leaving so soon?" came a breathless voice from behind me. I pivoted, just as her intoxicating scent wreathed my senses.

"Nyra! Should you not be halfway to the border by now?" I whispered as I drew closer to her cloaked figure. Despite my words, I felt happy to see her. I took her hand, and pressed a light kiss to the back of it.

She blushed, her lips parting in surprise, before she composed herself. "You should know I cannot be frightened away so easily."

"My father was serious. Every guard in Astoria will know your face by tomorrow."

"Then I will simply have to wear a different one." As I watched, the air shimmered around Nyra, and a stranger stood before me for a moment before the mirage faded.

I blinked. How had I not thought of that? "You are staying, then?"

"I refuse to return to my people empty-handed," Her mesmerizing gaze darkened, but she did not look away. As if she expected me to challenge her resolve.

"I understand, even if I disagree with your methods." I lifted a hand to her face, brushed my thumb against the hard set of her mouth until her lips softened.

"I..." Silent conflict raged behind her eyes, but she eventually spoke. "I am out of time, Orion. I just received word that the last oasis will be completely dry within a fortnight."

"So soon? I am sorry to hear that." The words felt hollow to my ears, but Nyra nodded all the same. "Could water be bartered from Harland?"

"The King of the Rocklands would not even accept our delegation." She said bitterly, biting her lip.

"And since neither the druids nor the witches care to interact with us humans, that only leaves Astoria," I mused.

"When I first heard of the power to grant wishes, I thought I had found the solution." Nyra laughed bitterly. "But it has proven more difficult than I anticipated to bend the ear of the king."

"Why have the tribes not sent an official diplomatic envoy?" I frowned. "Why go about this in such a round-about manner? My father would welcome such an outreach from the tribes—but all of this stirring of dissent during a crisis, the debacle tonight—it only hurts your cause!"

"After the Woman-King's attempt to establish a deal with both the witches and Harland fell through, the tribes believed sending another envoy would prove just as futile. They said it would be a grievous waste of time and resources, when we have so little left." Nyra scowled. "And your method seems to have been just as ineffective!"

"I was making great progress, Nyra! The first time I brought the subject up, he stormed out of the room. But more recently, he told me he would consider my proposal—that if he saw that the tribes were open to it, that they had let go of their pride and condescension towards him, an alliance might strengthen both of our countries!"

Her eyes went as wide as saucers. "He said that? And yet I...I almost exposed your secret tonight, after all you have done for me..." Nyra dropped her gaze, shame and frustration bowing her shoulders.

Despite the spike of alarm that rushed through me at her confession, I gently lifted her chin. "But you did not. You kept my secret." Her eyelashes fluttered delicately, and I felt a surge of protectiveness.

"I...It seems I have ruined our date," Nyra finally replied, her eyes rimmed with unshed tears.

"Tonight may have been a setback, but we must not give up. Tomorrow, I will speak with my father again, and even if that bears no fruit, once I have gathered enough starpower, I can try to summon a rainstorm, to buy more time. Even sending a caravan laden with waterskins to the desert is still an option.

"As for tonight, the night is still young! We have at least another hour before the starburst display begins. In the meantime, allow me to show you why I love this festival so much." I took her hand and led her deeper into the market.

Just because the night had gotten off to a rocky start did not mean it was too late to save it. I bought skewers of starfruit for us to enjoy as we watched the many performances occurring all throughout the city. Incredibly talented musicians, acrobats, and dancers displayed their skills, drawing appreciative crowds who showered them with praise and coins.

When we stumbled across a square filled with dancers moving to a lively tune, I took her in my arms and led her in our traditional folk dances. Though they were quite different from what she was used to, she caught on in no time. Tonight, we were not a prince and a refugee, but two people in love, happily lost in the crowd.

She even cheered for me when I entered a sprinting contest, giving me the boost I needed to win the short race. My prize was a wreath of fresh wildflowers. When I returned to where Nyra was waiting for me, I leaned down to give her a slight kiss on the lips. As I did, I slipped the wreath from my shoulders to hers, and she made a delighted little noise.

And then she wrapped her arms around my neck and returned the kiss—but with much more passion. I melted into her, spearing my hand through her thick, luscious hair as I pulled her close. Her lips tasted like the sweetest starfruit, and felt like the softest of silks.

As we broke apart, however, I thought I caught a glimpse of the strangest expression on her face. It was gone before I could begin to identify it.

"What happened to your necklace? The one you always wear under your tunic?"

Her question sent a ripple of unease through me. Most never noticed the amulet. Ah, perhaps she had noticed when she failed to cast mirage magic on me. She would have been searching for the starsteel that canceled out her magic.

"My...father is currently wearing it. It was my mother's originally, you see, and so there are times when my father likes to have it. Especially...around my birthday," I explained haltingly.

"Is your birthday near?" she asked.

"Tomorrow." I smiled tightly. "Tomorrow is both my birthday and the anniversary of my mother's death."

"I see." Nyra fell silent for a moment, as if deep in thought. "In that case, I want you to have this."

Nyra held out a small box. My fingers brushed hers as I took it, her warmth lingering. When I opened the box, I saw a pair of simple golden earrings that rested on a bed of velvet.

"I know it is not the custom for men here to pierce their ears, but in my culture, it is tradition to give these to someone you care for." My heart trilled at her words, at the way she was looking at me.

"Thank you." I said a tad huskily. Then I glanced around impulsively, and tugged Nyra towards the stall I had spotted. "I think I would like to wear them right away."

She laughed in surprise, and it was the work of a moment to pay the jewelry merchant to pierce my ears and add the golden rings to my earlobes. Much to my relief, I only felt a slight pinch, and the lingering soreness was far removed from the sorts of aches I acquired during a regular sparring session.

Though I might have some explaining to do when my father saw me. I would think about that later.

"They look wonderful on you, just as I thought." She traced her fingertips along the shell of my ear, and I resisted the urge to shudder.

"Thank you for the gift." I guided her lips to mine, losing my senses in her taste, her scent.

"Might I interest you in some rings?" The vendor suddenly asked. And we self-consciously broke apart.

As Nyra went to politely look at the wares the woman was gesturing to, I heard the bells begin to chime the hour, marking the beginning of a new day.

But before the bells had even finished ringing, I felt a surge of magic, as if I were wielding the amulet's power to grant a wish, just as I had every night around this time since I had saved Rigel. Even without the amulet, I could feel a well of starlight within me, deep in my core. It felt stronger tonight—perhaps because I was out under the stars, instead of cooped up in my office.

I moved to join Nyra, but froze as I passed one of the mirrors the vendor had attached to her stall. I watched in mounting horror as my blue eyes began to glow, and my hair faded from jet black to a glowing silvery-white. What was happening? I could not afford to let anyone see me like this!

I frantically glanced around, and quickly grabbed a hat from a neighboring stall that I could use to hide my hair. I tossed him a silver coin when he protested, which was likely twice what the hat was worth. I had to hide, before anyone noticed!

For a moment, I considered telling Nyra, but something held me back. What would I even tell her, when I myself had no clue what was happening to me?

"Nyra, I need to go. There is an emergency at the guild." I kept the brim tilted low over my face, and trained my eyes on her feet, which turned towards me as I spoke. "I am sorry I have to cut our date short, but I promise to make it up to you!"

As I turned and hurried away through the crowd, I heard her call out my name in confusion, but as much as it may have wounded her, I did not turn around.

I pulled out my starsteel watch before remembering it was drained of starlight, as I had been too busy over the last week to recharge it. But to my surprise, my touch brought it to life, and I was able to send a starnote as I stumbled through the crowded streets.

As soon as I could, I dove into a dark alley, and ran far faster than I had during that silly festival race all the way back to the guild house. I kept my hand on the hat, ensuring it was firmly on my head the entire time.

When I got to the guild, it appeared to be deserted. Of course, everyone was out and about, enjoying the festival. Like I should be. Oh, I hoped I had not come off as too cold by leaving so abruptly! But I would have to worry about that later.

I rushed inside, and slammed the door shut behind me. I leaned against the wood as I panted, my heart pounding in my ears. The rush of starlight within me gave no indication it would be subsiding anytime soon. Wisps of starlight wafted from my skin, brightening the air around me.

I needed help, and I hoped she had seen my starnote, that she had meant what she said to me the other day.

"Astrid!" I yelled out. "We have a problem!"

22

Astrid

"Orion, what is wrong? Has something happened?" I panted. I had arrived just before Orion burst through the door of the guild house.

It was so rare for Orion to send me a starnote first that I had left the others in Sirius' and Leo's care before racing back here. I had been under the impression that Orion would be acting as Prince Sterling throughout the Wish Festival, and that he would be watching the starbursts with Nyra instead of us. Jealousy twisted my insides at the thought.

So why was he here? I saw no sign of injury, though his face was partially hidden by a large hat he was wearing. Wait, why was he wearing a hat at night?

"Are we alone?" Orion glanced around the dark guild house.

"Everyone else is out enjoying the festival," I replied, a tad testily.

"Good." Orion's shoulders sagged. "Because I need your help, and I need you to keep this a secret from everyone." I had never seen him so jumpy and fidgety, even before a tavern brawl. And why was he avoiding my eyes?

He slowly reached up and removed the hat, his eyes finally finding mine. His *glowing* eyes. I gasped. His normally dark hair was also glowing a bright silver, and now that I was looking closer, I could see the wisps of starlight that were wafting from his skin. Though I could not see them, I had a feeling that the stars on his back were glowing as well.

"Did you grant a wish like last time?" I asked. Wait, since when did he have pierced ears?

Orion scowled. "No! And that is the problem! Not only did I *not* grant any wishes, but I do not even have the amulet that lets me do so!"

My eyes widened. If it were only the amulet that allowed him and the king to grant wishes, then how had he saved Rigel when the amulet was already spent? Orion froze, and raised a hand to his mouth. I realized he had not meant to say that last part.

"What do you mean, *like last time?*"

I blinked. "When you saved Rigel, your hair and eyes glowed just like this. I thought... Does this not happen every time you grant a wish?"

"No." He ran a hand through his silvery hair, causing a cascade of starlight to disperse into the air. "This has never happened before. And should not even be possible."

I stepped forward cautiously, and touched a lock of his hair, marveling at the way the starlight felt cool and tingly on my skin. Orion stiffened, but did not move away.

"Have you asked your father?"

"No." He waved a hand almost resentfully through the glimmering starlight that danced in the air around him.

"Perhaps he would know why this is happening to you. And...I think he would be proud of what you have accomplished with Hyperion...Prince Sterling," I whispered his name like a prayer and a curse. I had never dared to speak it aloud before.

He looked startled, and his gaze reluctantly found mine. "Are you... Are you upset?" Orion asked cautiously. He looked at me guardedly, as if he were bracing himself for the conversation we both had been dancing around and trying to avoid since that fight with Khalifon.

I took a deep breath, finally ready to take that plunge.

"Upset? I was incredibly upset. Orion—Sterling—whoever you are—you have been lying to me since the day we met. *Of course* I am upset!" The words burst out of me, giving voice to my pent-up frustrations. "How could you keep this from me?!"

A muscle feathered in his jaw. He looked away.

"I have been right by your side every step of the way, from founding Hyperion to every midnight emergency! I admired your mission, and wanted to help you save other people, just like you saved me! But beyond all of that, I...I wanted to stay by your side." A lump rose in my throat, and tears pricked the back of my eyes. "Did you honestly think your title would change any of that?" This time, I was the one who took a step back. His gaze snapped to mine.

He advanced for every step I took back, erasing the distance between us. Concern replaced the wariness in his mesmerizing eyes.

"I...I apologize for not telling you sooner." He raised a hand, as if to cup my face, but dropped it back to his side.

"Were you ever going to?" I whispered hoarsely, hugging my arms around myself. This was not how I had imagined this conversation going.

"I..." he trailed off. His silence was answer enough.

I turned my face away, disappointment licking at my heart.

"I have done everything you asked, supported you in any way I could. I told you I would lay down my life for you. What more do I have to do to earn your trust?" The words sounded broken and jagged, even to my ears.

This time, Orion took my hand, and waited for me to look at him. The starlight ringed his head like a halo, and I could not help but catch my breath.

"The last time I told someone the truth, when I was little...I was betrayed. Little did I know, he was a spy for the Kingdom of Harland, and he sold me out to them the same day. Their hired thugs kidnapped me, demanding a series of wishes in exchange for my life." He laughed humorlessly. "After that, I took up sword fighting. And I have feared revealing my secrets ever since."

"So that was how you wound up in Khalifon's cages with me." I squeezed his hand, despite myself. I hated picturing how badly the so-called friend must have hurt him, if that experience still affected him so deeply.

"I *do* trust you, Astrid, more than anyone else." He raised my hand to his lips and pressed a kiss to the back of it. "I am sorry my cowardice hurt you."

"You are far removed from being a coward." A liar, yes, but not a coward. My skin tingled where his lips had touched it, my pulse quickening. My ears warmed, even though I knew better than to read into the gesture. "Truthfulness aside, you are the bravest and most selfless person I know."

He chuckled. "Then I am sure you can guess why I cannot ask my father about this." He released my hand and gestured to his hair. My hand suddenly felt far too cold and empty.

I felt like I was treading on treacherous ground, exploring this new openness between us. At least the building sense of resentment and betrayal had finally eased, leaving my heart feeling lighter. But Orion's glowing gaze reminded me we still had a glaring problem to solve.

I frowned. "He does not know about Hyperion, does he?"

Orion shook his head. "He forbade me from using the amulet to grant wishes long ago. Hence the secrecy. If he discovered what I have been up to, that I have been 'borrowing' the amulet all this time... Well, suffice it to say I would not be permitted to set foot beyond the castle walls ever again."

I nodded slowly. It made sense that the king would not want to risk losing his son the way he had lost his wife. I pushed away the stab of guilt I felt.

"Hiding your activities may have just become nigh impossible, if this is going to happen every night now," I pointed out.

Orion groaned. "How can I possibly hide *this?* Wearing a hat at night is ridiculous, and it still cannot completely conceal the glow."

"What if I make you a wig? How do you feel about being a blonde?" I tried to keep a straight face, but my traitorous lips kept twitching.

Orion looked at me, raising one eyebrow. We stared at each other in silence for a moment before we both burst out laughing at the absurdity of the situation. It felt good to laugh, to ease the tension in the air.

A boom rang out, rattling the window panes.

"The starburst display must be starting," Orion breathed.

"Come on, we can watch them from the window in my workshop." Before I could think better of it, I grabbed his hand and towed him behind me.

I moved my chair out of the way and unlatched the window, swinging it wide so we could have an unobstructed view of the sky. The dark night was filled with stars, without a single cloud to dim their light. A flower of light bloomed in the darkness, followed by another loud boom as the petals of the flower cascaded into a shower of sparks that fizzled out long before they touched the ground.

More and more starbursts filled the heavens in a dazzling array of colors. Flares shot through the sky as well, mimicking shooting stars. It was a sight I never tired of seeing.

I glanced over at Orion, whose gaze was also riveted on the display. The starbursts were reflected in his eyes, his own inner starlight silvering the sharp planes of his face.

"What would you wish for?" I suddenly asked.

"What?" He turned to me, startled.

"You are always granting other people's wishes, but I have never heard you mention even once what it is that *you* want." This was something I had wanted to ask him for years. Whenever someone else had brought the subject up, he would always brush them off, changing the subject. "My only wish is one that can never be granted." A wistful look flitted across his features. "Not even the magic of the stars can bring my mother back."

"I am so sorry," I whispered, guilt clogging my throat.

"What for? It is not your fault." Orion smiled sadly.

Oh, if only he knew how wrong he was. Did I even have the right to feel hurt by the secrets he had kept from me, when I had yet to be fully honest with him? But if that tender expression soured to one of hatred when he looked at me, I would never be able to live with myself.

Even so, I was fiercely and selfishly glad that Orion was watching the starbursts here with me, instead of with Nyra.

"Though darkness falls..." I offered.

"Still the stars find their way," he answered with a soft smile.

23

Astrid

The starburst finale lit up the night, illuminating everything beneath it with splashes of bright colors. One final boom echoed through the air, and the final lightbloom fizzled out. Although I had seen the spectacle many times before, this was the first time I had watched it with just Orion.

And after the conversation we had just had, the way he had finally opened up and been honest with me for the first time... I felt closer than ever to him. Perhaps now was the time to share my own secrets.

Before I could work up the courage, Orion turned away from the window to scan the various vials, instruments, and coins that lay strewn haphazardly across my desk.

"How has your research been going? Have Nova and Castor been helpful?"

"They have both been a great help. They look at things in a way that I would never even consider, and thanks to that, and the desert herbs, I have started working on an improved remedy. The last one we concocted had some restorative effects, so I am hopeful this one will be an improvement upon it," I rambled. "Adding a few drops of liquid starlight seems to have boosted the effects of the other herbs. But using some in every dose would make the remedy far too costly, both to produce and to purchase."

"I convinced my father to put me in charge of the hunt for a cure," Orion revealed. "Spare no expense. The crown will bear the costs." Orion pulled out a coin purse and emptied it onto my desk, the gold and silver coins clattering onto the wood.

"Thank you. This will help," I murmured. Liquid starlight and the herbs I needed had become increasingly scarce and expensive as of late.

Orion's gaze snagged on a jar whose cork had come loose. When he went to pick it up, he accidentally knocked over one of the water samples I had been studying. I lurched to my feet as the liquid spread across the desk and dripped onto the floor. Fortunately, all of my herbs were safe in their own bottles. The coins could afford to get wet.

"Apologies," he said, pinching the bridge of his nose. "Lack of sleep must have made me clumsy."

"No harm was done," I reassured him as I took the handkerchief he offered and began to mop up the spillage. The circles under his eyes *were* more pronounced than usual. But at least his hair and eyes were slowly losing their glow.

He brought the bottle he had grabbed beneath his nose and sniffed. His brow scrunched in confusion. "Astrid, what are these sweet-smelling berries?"

I looked over at the bottle. "Sandberries. Nova was able to find a variety of effective herbs from the south to combat the plague, in addition to the ones Nyra suggested." The tribeswoman's name tasted sour on my tongue.

"So these are from the desert?" he clarified.

"Yes. They do have potent effects, but not the kind I was hoping for." I had mopped up most of the water, so I set the fabric aside to dry.

"What kind of effects?"

I pushed the bottle away from his nose, and popped the cork securely into place. "Sandberries have hypnotic properties. Their scent can cause people to become overly open to suggestion. With enough exposure, you could convince someone to do just about anything."

"But this is...this is what her perfume..." he muttered to himself.

I gasped, staring dumbfounded at my desk. Everything else faded away as the implications of what I was seeing hit me like a bolt of lightning from the blue.

"Orion," I hissed, my eyes riveted to my desk.

"Hmm?" He sounded distracted.

"Look at the silver coins."

"What about them?" He finally peered at them. "They are a tad tarnished, but that hardly seems like cause for alarm."

"They were not tarnished when you set them down." Even as I watched, the black discoloration was still spreading beneath the few water droplets I had failed to dry.

"Strange. But I still do not see—"

"Orion," I cut him off, slowly lifting my eyes to his. "The plague is not a naturally occurring sickness. It is a poison."

"What?" he croaked. His eyes widened.

Something thudded into the floor behind me. I turned to see Nova and Castor standing in the doorway, wearing twin expressions of shock on their faces. Castor had dropped a bag of sweets, but held his hands out as if he still held the parcel. They must have returned early from the festival.

I noticed Orion glance at his hair, and he let out a breath when he realized it was back to normal.

"The plague is a poison?" Nova looked sickened by the news.

"No wonder we had so much trouble trying to identify the cause, and how it was spreading. All this time, we have only been referencing *diseases*. I never even thought to check the symptoms against signs of poisoning," Castor muttered, more to himself than to us. I nodded.

"How do you know?" Orion stood from his chair. Tension crackled through the air like lightning.

"Silver turns black when touched by certain types of poisons," I explained, as I rushed over to the shelves in the corner. My two assistants followed at my heels like silent ghosts, all thoughts of celebration forgotten. I ran my fingers over each worn book spine until I found the one I was searching for. I pulled it out and laid it on the table, right next to the blackened coins, and flipped through its pages.

"Here." I pointed to one of the entries in the compendium. "Arsenic, commonly used to poison rodents, is difficult to detect in food. But when it comes in contact with silver, the metal will begin to tarnish almost immediately."

Orion leaned over my shoulder to scan the entry. Castor and Nova crowded around as well. "I was under the impression arsenic worked quickly. The plague victims sometimes lasted up to a week or two once symptoms appeared."

"What if everyone was exposed to different amounts? Some people have higher levels of tolerance, like how I get food poisoning easily but Nova has an iron stomach," Castor suggested.

"That could be a part of it, but..." I thought for a moment, and was struck by an idea. I pulled out my starsteel watch and touched the casing to a drop of water on the coin. The metal brightened.

"There is more than just arsenic," I breathed. "There is magic in the poison."

"Is it the work of the witches?" Orion growled, his expression darkening. I saw a hint of the prince beneath the guildmaster, reacting to a threat to his people. I had never seen him look so serious.

My eyes fell on the bottle of sandberries. Seeing the direction of my gaze, Nova flipped to the section of the book on poisons from the desert. She skimmed through the entries until she found an illustration of a snake with pale gold scales.

Orion sucked in a breath.

"Sandvipers use mirage magic to hide themselves or distract their prey while hunting. And eating these snakes is how the tribespeople were rumored to have acquired their own mirage magic," Nova read aloud. "Their venom acts slowly, causing a weakness of the limbs and dark bruises to appear on the skin. A paste composed of the stems and leaves of the Moringa and Ceiba plants are the most effective antidotes, outside of liquid starlight."

"Those are the symptoms all right," Orion said grimly.

"Normally, ingesting the venom would not be a problem, unless there was a cut in the mouth," I mused. "But if the magic-imbued venom were combined with one or more other poisons..."

"Where was that water sample from?" Orion demanded.

"The well near the orphanage," Castor replied softly, his eyes on the near-empty vial. "Most of the samples were from nearby—the working districts."

"It was never contagious. Our wells were poisoned." Nova raised a hand to cover her mouth. Castor laced his fingers through hers, and she leaned against him, as if all her strength had abandoned her.

"Only the wealthy can afford to drink wine, or from private wells," Castor said grimly. "Which is why none of them showed the signs."

"Nova, Castor." I handed them the open book, pointing to the sandviper entry. "I need you to get as much of these herbs and liquid starlight as you possibly can. We need to make as many antidotes as we can, as soon as possible."

Excitement and intense relief buzzed through me at this revelation. I could *finally* create a cure for this horrible disease—no, horrible poison—that had nearly stolen my dear students from me. And that meant Orion would no longer have to bleed himself dry and risk his life to save the victims!

Nova clutched the book to her chest, her horrified expression turning into one of determination. Castor grabbed the untarnished coins from the pile on the desk and slipped them into his pocket.

"You can count on us," Castor declared, a determined set to his chin. At my nod, they both ran out the door and back into the night. Several of the apothecaries should still be open, since it was a festival night.

Once they were gone, I turned to Orion as the full implications of this discovery dawned on me. "This was intentional. But why bother causing such suffering among those who hold no power? Why not target those in the castle?" I locked gazes with Orion.

He blanched. "Most of Astoria's soldiers and guards come from the working districts."

I gasped, as all of the pieces clicked into place. "An invasion. The tribes are going to invade—no, they have already begun!" It all suddenly made sense—the massive influx of refugees, their fixation on wishes...everything!

"No, we cannot know that!" Orion protested. He scowled, and I could practically see the gears turning in his head.

"Think about it! Their oases have all dried up, but Astoria is filled with water and natural resources. *One* of our lakes is larger than all of their oases combined!" I ground my teeth as Orion shook his head in disbelief.

I knew why he was refusing to accept this. This was all about *her*. But I had to make him see reason!

"The tribesmen and women have been sowing discontent, riling up people's fears and selling phony cures to the poison they created!" I practically shouted. "Even tonight, they caused a scene!"

"No. No! She—they would never do that!" Orion shook his head in denial, but I could see the uncertainty in his eyes.

"Orion—no, Prince Sterling." His eyes snapped to mine. "Is there *anything* you would not do for your kingdom, your people?" I asked with deadly quiet, changing tact.

"...No."

"There. You have your answer, even if you are too afraid to admit it." A muscle feathered in his jaw. "And Nyra is a part of it."

Orion stiffened, but did not deny it this time. His gaze landed on the sandberries. "Every time I saw her, after that night when I revealed who I was, she always smelled like sandberries." The agony on his face nearly ripped my heart in two.

"You mean...?" I trailed off, horror and hope waging war within me.

"She used me. Manipulated me." His hands clenched into fists at his sides, and his head hung low. Orion looked utterly defeated.

"After tonight, they have little hope of being granted a wish peacefully. If the purpose behind the poison was to weaken our defenses, both within and without, that could mean..." I trailed off.

Horror dawned on Orion's face. His hands went slack at his sides.

"There are hardly any guards at the castle tonight, and most of the able-bodied ones are out patrolling the festival, in case of more unrest. It is practically unguarded." Orion's expression became bleak. "Nyra knows that I am the prince. She knows what I look like. And she can use her mirage magic to look just like me..."

"Does she know about the amulet?" I went still.

The prince froze, his eyes slowly finding mine. "I think she does."

"Do you have it with you?" I asked quietly, already fearing the answer.

"No, my father does. And tonight, he is practically unguarded."

24

Orion

"I have to go back." A sense of nausea roiled in my stomach. It had to be a lie. It *had* to. But the sandberries... Had Nyra truly been deceiving me this whole time? I had been so *sure* we both wanted the same things, even if the way we went about achieving them was different.

But I needed to check for myself. So long as nothing was amiss, I could simply ask Nyra to explain.

"I am coming with you." Astrid pinned me with her gaze, daring me to argue. Her chin had that stubborn set to it that meant there was no changing her mind.

I gave a jerky nod, and she lifted her bow and quiver from where they hung on the wall. She would never be allowed past the gate with a weapon under normal circumstances, but would be permitted inside if she were with me. A chill ran down my spine. Someone who looked like me could easily infiltrate the castle, even with a group of armed warriors.

Was there a reason beyond the one Nyra had given me for her to stay in Astoria, despite the commotion she had caused tonight? I wanted so badly to believe that this was all a huge misunderstanding. The odds of the second person I had trusted with my identity acting the same as the first were slim...right?

As we left the guild behind and pushed our way through the crowded streets, I watched Astrid pull out her starsteel watch and send off a few starnotes. But I was too distracted by my scattered thoughts to notice more than that.

My elation at discovering a cure for the plague had been completely overshadowed by the revelation that it was a manufactured poison. With everything in me, I desperately wanted to believe that Nyra had no hand in this. That she had no knowledge of what her fellow refugees had done and were doing to my homeland in the name of their own. But Astrid's words echoed in my mind like a warning knell: Was there anything I would not do for my kingdom? Was there anything Nyra would not do for hers?

My heart and my mind warred with each other, my thoughts a reflection of the jumbled crowds around us, filled with light and laughter, all blissfully unaware of the crisis bearing down on them. Long before I could make any sense of my racing thoughts, we arrived at the castle gates.

"Halt! Identify yourselves!" ordered one of the guards.

I pulled back the hood of my cloak.

"Your Highness!" The guard bowed. "Please, forgive me for not recognizing you." Then he paused, eyeing Astrid. "And is she...?"

"Astrid is my guest. She is to be treated with the utmost respect," I said by way of explanation. Neither of the two guards were injured, though they both had strange looks on their faces, as if they had seen a ghost.

"Prince Sterling! I did not expect you to return so soon," Rigel greeted me as he approached from behind with another pair of guards. He must just be returning from patrolling the festival.

But the confused and dazed looks on the gate guards' faces held my attention. Unease blossomed in the pit of my stomach, and I had the horrible feeling that this was the calm before the storm.

"What troubles you?" I asked them. An achingly sweet, familiar scent wafted from them both.

"I...when did you..." one guard stuttered. "I could have sworn I just let you through the gates not thirty minutes ago, Your Highness. Just after the last shift change."

I blanched, glancing at Astrid. Her face had gone equally pale. My hand strayed to my sword, and Rigel tensed.

Nyra was already inside the castle.

"Was he—I mean, I—alone, when you let me in earlier?" I demanded, advancing on the guard. There was an unfocused look about his eyes that made me uncomfortable.

"No, you had several guards with you." He paused, as if he was having difficulty remembering the details. "For some reason, I cannot recall their names, or what they looked like."

How much sandberry did it take to make a man this placid? Nyra must have been practically swimming in the stuff. My skin crawled as I briefly wondered exactly how much she had used on *me.*

I felt like a fool. A soft, trusting *fool.*

Ice ran through my veins, my pulse slowing to a crawl before thundering into a gallop. The tribesmen were already within the castle.

"Recall every guard out on patrol. Lock down the castle—allow no one in or out!" I commanded.

"Understood, Your Highness!" Both guards bowed, before one ran off to spread the order. The two that came with Rigel jumped to obey my order at a nod from the knight.

I ran into the castle, Astrid and Rigel keeping pace on either side. As we sprinted through the halls, servants jumped out of the way, gaping at me in surprise at my un-princely garb and behavior. My eyes darted this way and that, all of my senses on high alert.

How many magic wielders were already within the castle? Once inside, they could have let even more inside, in the guise of more guards or servants. They could be anyone, and the only way to tell for sure that mirage magic was not being used was to touch a piece of starsteel to their skin. Which we clearly did not have time for.

"What is happening?" Rigel demanded as he dodged a decorative suit of armor and clipped a tapestry.

"The plague is a magic-infused, man-made poison from the desert," Astrid explained, but I cut her off.

"Rigel, how would you defend against a people who can use magic to look like anyone they have ever seen before?"

He went silent, then swore so colorfully even Astrid appeared impressed. His mind had always been as sharp as his blade. "The guards let in someone who looked like you, but was in fact someone else?"

"Yes."

"The tribesmen call it mirage magic," Astrid added.

"I need to summon the rest of the knights—" Rigel started.

"No! Not when we have no idea how many of them are already inside the castle. You could be surrounding us with enemies for all we know." I took a sharp left, narrowly avoiding knocking over a decorative vase.

"Is there no flaw in the magic? No way to tell?" Rigel huffed.

"The voice will be different. But the only way to dispel the illusion is to touch starsteel to their skin."

"Blade to the throat. Got it." Rigel now eyed everyone we passed with suspicion. I appreciated how quick he was to catch on.

We rounded the final turn and sprinted down the hall towards my father's study. My stomach dropped to my toes when I saw Rigel's father, Sir Magnus, lying in front of the open wooden doors. His unseeing eyes stared straight through me, his greatsword still clutched in his hand.

Rigel made a choked sound at the sight, as did I. Memories flashed through my mind of how many happy days we had spent together in the training hall. He had been like a second father to me, and the one who had made time for me when my own could not. Rarely had he refused my childish requests to play games, when I was little and alone, and his great booming laugh had helped fill the empty hole in my heart that my mother had left. When I grew older, our play had turned into practice, and he had drilled me endlessly on how a knight must never let go of his sword, no matter what. Even death had not stolen that dedication from him.

He had died as he had lived: With a sword in his hand.

A lump rose in my throat, and I could not tear my eyes away from his. When was the last time I had sparred with him? Laughed with him? Why had I not made some time for him, as he had for me, despite my busy schedule? Now, it was too late—I had squandered that chance, and never again would I have it.

I silently gripped Rigel's stiff shoulder.

A clatter sounded from inside the room, snapping me out of my daze and reminding me that Sir Magnus never strayed far from my own father's side.

I drew my sword as I burst through the door, the slither of starsteel beside me indicating Rigel had done the same, putting his duty above his grief. My heart ached for him, even as I took reassurance from his steadfast presence. My eyes were immediately drawn to the two people silhouetted by the roaring fire in the study's hearth, and I skidded to a halt in shock at the scene before me. My father stood, holding out a wrapped present to a person who looked for all the world just like me, with a handful of guards standing like statues in the shadowy recesses of the room.

I watched with mounting horror as the perfect copy of me drew his weapon and plunged an iron scimitar into my father's chest. The copy grinned at the expression of disbelief on the king's face, and cruelly twisted the blade.

I froze in disbelief, rooted to the spot. I could not tear my eyes away. Time slowed, and a terrible silence roared in my head. An empty chasm yawned wide in my chest, threatening to swallow me and my weak starlight whole.

"Father, no!" I screamed.

He slowly turned to look at me. The shock on his familiar features rapidly shifted to confusion, and then understanding and something akin to relief.

"Sterling, my little star," he rasped. Blood trickled from the corner of his mouth. He lifted a trembling hand in my direction, as if to give me the wrapped package it held. My birthday gift.

My heart splintered.

Time sped up, and my evil twin tore the sword from the only family I had left, his precious blood staining his impeccably clean leather armchair, the one where he had sat me in his lap and told me tales of the stars when I was little. The cruel grin seemed so foreign on my face. As the king fell beneath the portrait of his queen, the copy snatched the star sapphire amulet from around his neck, snapping the delicate chain.

The mirage rippled upon contact with the starsteel, which quickly stripped away every last shred of the illusion. My heart shattered at what it revealed.

Looming over my father's body, his blood dripping from her iron scimitar, stood Nyra.

25

Orion

Nyra really *had* betrayed me. She had *used* me. All of that time spent together, the way she had smiled at me...all of it had been a lie, a ruse.

I watched in numb disbelief as Tariq, along with two other tribesmen, stepped out of the shadows, their disguising illusions fading away. The dancing firelight made their smug expressions look monstrous.

I realized distantly that this was what Tariq had meant by his threat.

Tariq sidled up to Nyra and kissed her. The other two pressed kisses to her hands, her arms. Nyra smiled indulgently, and waved them off. They jumped at her silent command, settling into a fighting stance and drawing their own scimitars.

I suddenly recalled that in the tribelands, it was not uncommon for a man to have a harem of women, instead of devoting himself entirely to only one, as we did in Astoria. Based on what I just witnessed, Nyra had a harem of her own highly-trained warriors.

I felt like I had been gutted, my heart ripped from my chest and crushed into a million little splinters.

It felt as if I were nine once more, crying out to my best friend for help as Khalifon and his men bound and gagged me. I was thrown over one man's shoulders like a sack of potatoes, to be used as a living bargaining chip against the king who had already lost his wife. And as I was hauled away, my betrayer grinned as one of the men dumped a pouch of gold into his waiting hands.

What a fool I had been. Had I not learned my lesson the first time? *This* was what trusting others got me.

My gaze drifted to my father's prone form, and I saw the slightest rise of his chest. *He was still alive!* An ember of hope flared to life in my chest. If I could just get to him, if I could steal just a few moments to utter the words...

Even without the amulet, perhaps I could save him, the way I had saved Rigel!

"We're the same, you and I," Nyra said softly as she looked down her nose at me. "We'd both do *anything* for our people. But I refuse to hold another loved one in my arms as they die from dehydration. So I will be taking your kingdom, Prince Sterling—or should I say, Orion?"

"He is nothing like you, you snake!" Astrid piped up angrily. Nyra sneered at her.

"Kill them." Nyra flicked a hand in our direction dismissively, her attention falling to the gleaming star sapphire she still gripped in one hand.

"Forever reigns the Woman-King!" chanted the three men as they lunged for us.

Nyra was the Woman-King?

I intercepted Tariq as he swung at Astrid, the coward. Sparks flew as our blades clashed, a deafening screech filling the air. Rigel engaged the other two, forcing him to stay on the defensive. I heard more than saw Astrid nock an arrow, and I heaved against Tariq, pushing him back, so she would have a clear shot at one of the two fighting Rigel.

"I have wanted to slice you open from nose to navel since the moment I first laid eyes on you!" grunted Tariq.

"I could say the same!" I growled back.

I parried his heavy blow, my arm aching from the impact. I thrust my sword at his unprotected chest, but he recovered in time to block. He feinted to the right, but I guarded my left as he whipped his scimitar around. The man was at least as skilled as Rigel, but I had seen such tricks before.

"How does it feel to be used by a woman?" Tariq slashed at my chest, and I jumped back, bumping into Astrid.

Her shot went wide, missing the tribesman.

"Do tell! I could not determine whether you were her lover or her manservant!" I lunged forward, forcing him back.

I did not have time for this—I had to get to my father! I only had a small window of opportunity before even starlight would be powerless to save him. And this hulking foreigner stood in my way!

I heard a cry as Astrid's second arrow struck true, downing one of Rigel's two opponents. Tariq looked over, distracted by the noise, and I used that opportunity to drive my starsword into his chest.

Tariq looked down in shock, his scimitar clattering to the hardwood floor. I wrenched my blade free and sprinted to my fallen father, even as Nyra's shriek rent the air.

"Tariq!" she screamed as she ran to him.

I dropped to my knees beside him, taking his limp hand in mine and placing the other over his wound, to try and stanch the flow. His face was already pale, the warmth in his strong hands giving way to ice.

"Father, I am here," I rasped, refusing to let the pricking behind my eyes turn into tears.

"I am...so proud of you, son." A cough racked his frame, causing blood to leak from beneath my trembling fingers. "Here...your birthday present."

How could he think of my birthday at a time like this? As if anything could possibly be more important than the simple presence of my father. Nevertheless, I took the small but infinitely precious gift from his shaking hand, and quickly tucked it into my pocket to appease him.

"All I need is you! Please, stay with me," I begged him, even as I closed my eyes and dug deep into my core, searching for that well of power that had healed Rigel's mortal wound. "Please, you cannot leave me here alone!"

"I will...watch over you, always," he wheezed. I felt the thrum of starpower flood my veins, felt it saturate my body, lighting the stars on my back and turning my hair to silver. "So you do...take after...your mother. Oh, I am so happy...that I will finally...see her again."

"I wish—" The words morphed into a cry of pain as an iron scimitar slashed across my left leg.

I opened my eyes and half-turned to see a tear-streaked and enraged Nyra preparing to strike me down, shattering my concentration like she had shattered my heart. Tariq had slumped against the wall behind her.

I rolled under my father's sturdy desk just in time, and heard splinters fly as her scimitar bit into the wood.

"How dare you do that to Tariq!" she yelled.

"How could you do this to me?! I trusted you! How could you betray me like this?!" I hurled back at her as I rolled to my feet. I glanced at where my starsword lay beside my father.

Nyra saw where I was looking and smirked as the air shimmered, and suddenly I was facing five Nyras instead of one. My gaze darted to Tariq, with whom Nyra must have left the starsteel amulet. I cursed under my breath.

"My people are *dying* of thirst! If your magic is not strong enough to revitalize the oases, then I will just have to bring my people here instead, to the land of water and stars." She and all her copies mirrored my movements, keeping their scimitars leveled at my chest. The copies kept switching places, so I could no longer tell which was the real one.

"And that gives you the right to poison my people, so you can steal the land?!" I saw all of the copies' eyes widen a fraction before they narrowed, as if she was shocked I had figured it out.

"You and your people are soft," she hissed, making no attempt to deny the accusation. "You do not deserve such luxury while my people suffer."

Who was this viper, who had replaced the sweet and shy Nyra? Or was this her true personality shining through her mirage of deceit?

"The tribes spurned our offers of alliance and aid," I spat, subtly edging closer to my father and my sword. Rigel was still battling his own foe: No aid would be coming from him.

"Too little, too late," she snarled as she advanced. "It was far easier to infiltrate your lax little kingdom, to spread poison and stir up some discontented ingrates, until the idea of a new king no longer sounded so unpleasant. Once I start granting all of their wishes, they will welcome me with open arms!"

"They will never bow to a tyrant!" Just a few more steps...

"They will bow, or they will die!" Nyra raged.

"Then you do not deserve them!" I lunged for my sword, ducking phantom blades.

The real one nicked my arm as I dove for my starsword and rolled to my feet. I slashed my weapon through the closest Nyra, and upon contact with the metal, the illusion dissipated like mist.

One of Astrid's arrows whizzed through another Nyra, the starsteel arrowhead neutralizing the copy. Now only three copies remained. I glanced back at Rigel, and saw him backing his opponent into a corner, one of Astrid's arrows embedded in the tribesman's shoulder.

Just when it seemed we had hope of turning the tide, there was a flash of starlight behind me, and I risked a glance to see Tariq lumbering to his feet, the telltale wisps of starlight still hovering around his healed wound. *That* was going to be a problem. And to make matters worse, a new group of tribesmen rushed into the cramped room, bloodstains on their brightly-colored clothes.

"Your Majesty!" cried a group of knights as they barged through the door, right behind the tribesmen. They took one look at the gruesome scene and rushed forward to meet the tribesmen with starsteel blades drawn. "Protect the king!"

I looked to my father. He lay completely still, his unseeing blue eyes, so like mine, trained on the portrait of his wife. I was struck by a bolt of visceral agony unlike anything I had ever known.

I was too late.

With a horrible shock, I realized the knights were not referring to my father. They meant *me*.

My father was gone.

I was now the King of Astoria.

One of the copies swung her scimitar at my neck, and it was only instinct honed over years of training that saved me. I brought my guard up just in the nick of time. Finally, I had found the real one.

I delivered a flurry of blows that Nyra somehow managed to block. Her skill with the blade surprised me, but only because I still saw the Nyra I knew where the Woman-King now stood.

I parried her next blow, ignoring the illusions that tried to distract me. I nearly lost my grip on my sword, and frowned when I realized I was having trouble curling my fingers. What was wrong with my hand?

The cut on my arm throbbed, and I looked down to see a purple bruise spreading around the wound.

Nyra's weapon was coated in poison.

"How do you like the effects of the undiluted poison?" She laughed at my expression.

I growled in frustration and rage, bringing up my guard as Nyra came at me with renewed vigor. What a cowardly tactic. Perfectly suitable for a traitorous snake like her.

It was all I could do to defend against her onslaught. My arm was going numb, a sensation that was rapidly encroaching on my chest. How long did I have until the poison reached my heart?

Darkness licked at the edges of my vision, and I stumbled. My strength fled my limbs, sapped by the encroaching poison. It seemed I would be seeing my parents much sooner than I had expected.

I only hoped Astrid and Rigel escaped.

Our blades screeched against one another, and with a flourish Nyra flung my sword from my stiff and unresponsive fingers. The world spun, the number of Nyras before me doubling before returning to normal. Sweat beaded on my skin as it heated up, the stars on the right side of my back transforming into burning pinpricks of light as they fought the poison and its foreign magic.

Which would prove stronger—the magic of the stars or the desert?

I staggered, and Nyra swept my legs out from under me. I fell to my knees, defeated and prone before my betrayer, as she leveled her iron scimitar at my neck.

26

Astrid

I drew back my arrow, aimed, and fired at a tribesman who was overpowering one of the knights. He moved as my arrow took flight, and it buried itself in his shoulder instead of his heart. I cursed under my breath.

I had gotten rusty.

Or perhaps it was the infernal smell of the sandberries that lay so heavily in the air. The sickly-sweet scent made it difficult to focus. Was *that* how Nyra had managed to wrap Orion around her little finger? With sandberry perfume?

A flash of light blinded me, and as I blinked the stars from my vision, I saw Tariq lumber back to his feet, Orion's amulet clutched in his hand. A black, star-shaped mark had appeared on his forehead.

I fired off another arrow as I took stock of the battle. The tribesmen were fierce fighters, and although our reinforcements had arrived just in time, we were still fighting an uphill battle. With Tariq back in action, those odds had only worsened.

If only Sirius, Leo, and Noctus were here!

A flurry of movement by the fireplace caught my attention, and I watched in horror as Orion fell. By the stars, how was it possible that Nyra had overpowered him, even with those magic copies? I had seen Orion sparring with my guildmates enough to know he was incredibly skilled.

My heart pounded in my ears when I spotted the discolored cut on his upper arm. The bruising looked exactly like the plague symptoms. Then it hit me: Nyra's blade was poisoned with a substance far more potent than what had already stolen so many lives.

It was so like her to use dirty tricks to the very end.

Orion's time was now limited. My eyes darted to the amulet Tariq still held. Could Orion heal himself like he had healed Rigel? Or did he need the amulet? Could we get him to the antidote Nova and Castor were concocting before the poison reached his heart?

My dislike of Nyra ballooned into hatred. Even though a small part of me felt vindicated by my misgivings about Nyra, now that she had shown her true colors, the rest of me hated to see Orion's hopes crushed. Because my world would be crushed alongside his.

"I had planned to offer you a place in my harem," Nyra purred, lifting Orion's chin with the point of her blade. Her eyes rested on his still-glowing hair, the silver light sharpening her cruel smile. "But I have a feeling you would be more trouble than you are worth. Things would have been much easier if that buffon Khalifon had succeeded in capturing you alive, but I have become accustomed to cleaning up after my men."

Khalifon had been working for Nyra?!

Nyra raised her scimitar high, preparing to strike Orion down. Time seemed to slow, as if everyone in this room was moving through thick molasses. The sounds of battle faded into the background, my world narrowing to the figures in front of me. I nocked another arrow, drawing the bowstring back with trembling fingers.

I could not afford to miss. But all three copies were about to swing at Orion's head. How could I know which one to aim for? The wrong choice would destroy Orion. And it would destroy me.

A sad smile curled my lips. Breaking the oath I had sworn to my mother on her deathbed would seal my fate, the one she had tried so valiantly to save me from. But my precious eighteen years of life had been borrowed time from the beginning.

As I had received, so I would give. After all, I had been truthful when I told Orion I would lay down my life for him.

I reached for the dormant magic in my veins, instinctively calling it forth for the first time in my life. It was sluggish, like a seedling under the first sunbeams of spring. But it did as I asked, traveling through my arm and into the shaft of the arrow, stopping just short of the starsteel tip. I told the wild magic of nature, of all living things, to seek the warm life of the tribeswoman, to ignore the lifeless copies and guide the arrow to her true body. As life called to life.

I let the arrow fly, even as darkness flashed across my vision, my body throbbing violently as the curse came roaring back to life, breaking free of the thin starlight restraint that had grown so brittle over time. The malicious magic stole my breath with its ferocity, my heart screaming in pain every time I tried to suck down some air.

The pain subsided nearly as quickly as it had come, leaving a dull ache behind. My sight cleared in time for me to see my arrow lodge in the chest of the true Nyra, my wild magic completing its mission. The two mirages fizzled out as the starsteel did its work, and the force of the blow knocked Nyra back, a deliciously startled and pained look on her face.

"Rigel!" I screamed. We had to get Orion out of here, but I knew I was not strong enough to carry him myself.

The knight finished off his opponent in one fluid motion. He sheathed his sword and sprinted for Orion, scooping him up and throwing him over his shoulder. The faithful knights on our side held off the other tribesmen as Rigel ran for the door. I ran with him, laying down cover with a spray of arrows to keep any tribesmen from getting close.

Tariq made as if to intercept Rigel, but changed course when he saw that Nyra had slumped against a bookcase, her blood staining the leather-bound tomes and her chest struggling to rise. Silvery starlight suffused the air as he began to stutter out a wish while holding the amulet over her wound. Blinding white light flashed as I followed Rigel out of the room. I cursed, knowing Tariq had used the amulet to save Nyra, just as she had used it to save him.

Until we stole the amulet back, it would be nigh impossible to defeat her. But we would have to worry about that later—right now, we had to focus on getting Orion the antidote before it was too late.

Rigel and I sprinted through the halls, dodging friend and foe alike. I kept my bow at the ready, firing off shots with my dwindling number of arrows at anyone who came too close. I trusted no one but my guildmates with his life. I whipped out my watch and sent a starnote before I glanced over to see Orion's eyelids fluttering closed, his breaths labored.

"Orion, do not dare close your eyes!" I shouted at him, before addressing Rigel. "We cannot let him fall asleep, or he may never wake again!"

Rigel led the way through the castle and into the guards' barracks, where we slipped through the servant's door and beyond the walls just as the warning bells began to toll. Rigel continuously pinched and slapped Orion's legs, startling him awake every time he began to go limp.

A shadow peeled off from an alleyway and joined my side, his throwing knives downing the three tribesmen who had evaded my arrows to follow us.

"Noctus, do they have it ready?" I gasped out as we sprinted across the cobblestones and into the crowded festival, where clueless subjects still milled about. My legs were burning, adding to the ache from the curse.

"It should be done by the time we get there." His eyes scanned our surroundings, constantly on high alert for new threats, a task made more challenging by the throngs of people.

The flight to the guild house from the castle was the most excruciating of my life. I pushed myself harder, faster, than I ever had before. I should have asked Sirius to train me more frequently when I had the luxury of time. I fell behind Rigel and Noctus, but I kept my eyes trained on Orion. I refused to be the reason we did not make it back in time. Every second was precious. Every second counted.

It was a small mercy when Sirius joined us as we left the more crowded market streets and plunged into the quieter sections of the merchant district. He swept me into his arms when he saw how I was flagging, falling ever further behind the others. All I could do was nod my thanks and grit my teeth against the pain in my muscles and from the curse as he carried me the rest of the way to our home. I prayed to the stars that Nova and Castor would have a viable antidote ready by the time we arrived.

Noctus threw open the doors as we rushed inside and barricaded them behind us. Rigel staggered to one of the treatment rooms, and I noticed for the first time that he was injured, with cuts in his arms and legs where his leather armor did not cover him. But he laid an unconscious Orion down on the bed with the utmost care before he collapsed against the wall, completely spent.

Nova and Castor ran into the room, and Nova handed me a vial filled with a silvery liquid as Sirius set me down beside Orion, whose breaths were becoming more labored. He must have passed out just before we arrived at the guild, which meant we were nearly out of time.

"We added all of the herbs the book mentioned into a whole vial of liquid starlight," Nova said. When her gaze fell on Orion, she started to tremble. "Will he…?"

"Good job, you two." I ruffled Nova's hair and nodded to Castor, who put his arm around Nova.

"What happened to him?" Sirius asked as everyone gathered around.

"Nyra betrayed him and killed the king." Sirius swore, as did Leo.

Noctus blanched. He alone understood the gravity of that statement. "That means…"

"If I cannot counteract this poison, Astoria will have no king, and the Kingdom of the Stars will have fallen completely," I said grimly as I popped off the cork and sat down on the bed beside the prince.

Stunned silence met my words. Everyone looked at each other in shock. We were all in danger now because of Orion's secret, and they had the right to know why.

"Orion is actually…?" Sirius trailed off in disbelief.

"Yes," Noctus answered his unspoken question.

Orion's eyelids fluttered once more and he moaned. I noted that the discoloration had reached his throat. Time was up. But by sacrificing just a little more of my own time, I might be able to save him.

I reached again for that wild magic that felt so foreign and yet so familiar, commanding it to bend to my will once more. It writhed in my grip, yearning to be set loose. I forced it through my arm and into the potion I held in my hand. I had no idea if this would work, but if druids could make a tree grow from an acorn into a towering oak, then surely I could imbue that same overflowing power into the antidote. My ears felt pinched and my skin began to glow with golden light as my magic flooded into the crushed herbs in the liquid antidote, enhancing their potency beyond their natural limits, making them three times as effective.

I just had to hope it would be enough.

Since he could not afford to lose a single drop, I tipped the precious concoction into my own mouth. I caressed Orion's face as I placed my lips over his, and made sure he swallowed every last drop.

I had never imagined my first kiss would be like this.

I slowly drew back, shuddering as the backlash from the curse hit me. I watched with a sort of numb detachment as the tips of my hair turned black, all the life and color leached out of it.

"Get me another bottle of starlight," I ordered Castor. He ran to my workshop as I pulled out my starsteel watch and pressed it to his discolored skin. "All of you, put as much starsteel as you can find on his skin. That will help cut through the magic in the poison."

The others did as I asked, and I watched with bated breath as the dark bruises slowly began to lighten. It was working!

His hair, which had faded back to black, began to glow silver again as the liquid starlight and antidote burned away the desert poison. My guildmates stared in shock at what they were seeing, at the wisps of starlight wafting from their guild master and sovereign.

Once all of the dark marks on his skin had completely vanished, Orion's breathing eased, his rigid muscles finally relaxing in peaceful sleep. I sat back and heaved a sigh of relief.

The antidote had worked.

Orion would live.

"Where do we go from here?" Sirius asked quietly, Estelle clinging to his leg. He put a hand on her thin shoulder.

I looked down at Orion wistfully, brushing a lock of his silvery hair from his forehead. As much as it scared me, I knew nothing would be the same again. The life of a simple herbalist and guild member that I had loved so dearly was over, now that Nyra ruled Astoria.

But so long as Orion was still with me, I knew I could face whatever came next. Whether that meant fleeing the kingdom or retaking it, I would stay by his side. For however long I had left.

"That is entirely up to King Sterling."

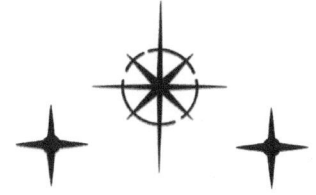

The Adventure Continues...

Orion and Astrid's adventure continues in The Druid Queen, which is available on Amazon here.

If you enjoyed The Starborn Prince, I would be forever grateful if you would leave it a review on Amazon here! Reviews make such a huge difference, and I love hearing from my readers!

Want Extra Content?

If you would like to order bookish merch, see character art, and receive updates, free book and audiobook announcements, and release notifications for new book, please sign up here:

Also by K. S. Gerlt

The Werewolf's Mask Series
The Werewolf's Mask

Daughter of Wind and Moonlight

Son of Fang and Fury

Daughter of Steel and Strife

Son of Prejudice and Pride

The Werewolf's Mask Series Coloring Book

The Kingdom of the Stars Series
The Starborn Prince

The Druid Queen

The Wish King

The Witch Queen

About the Author

K. S. Gerlt is an award-winning artist and the author of The Werewolf's Mask series. An avid reader herself, she has always loved diving into the magical worlds within books, from the classics to modern fantasy and adventure. She grew up in Southern California, where her pastimes include horseback riding, ice skating, and painting.